RUB-A-DUB-DUB
DEATH IN A TUB

FRAN HAGAMAN

Requests for such permission should be addressed to:
Loch Wohl Press,
78 Erie Stree.
Shreveport, LA 71106

Hagaman, Frances E.
        Rub-A-Dub-Dub, Death in a Tub

Cover Design: Manjari Graphics
Layout: J. L. Saloff

Print book ISBN: 978-0-9749649-4-2
Ebook ISBN: 978-0-9749649-1-1

Second edition: v. 2.01

To:
Van Hagaman
best friend and loving husband

ACKNOWLEDGMENTS

The author gratefully acknowledges the kind assistance she has received from the following:

Ronnie Walsh who deciphered the handwritten manuscript

Tom Bird for helping release the author within

Russell Thompson Gulf Coast resource person

Sergeants Rickey Scroggins and Mike Day – Shreveport Police Department.

Joe and Barbara Manno – forensic toxicologists

Susan M. Kelly – editorial assistance

S. K. Garner; Evelyn Still – copyediting

Manjari Henderson – cover design

Jamie Saloff – book layout and design

The multitude of friends, pharmaceutical representatives, associates, faculty members at LSU health science center-Shreveport, and the staff of Region VII Office of Mental Health-Louisiana.

RUB-A-DUB-DUB
DEATH IN A TUB

FRAN HAGAMAN

LOCH WOHL PRESS

ONE

Heat shimmered on the distant gray Gulf as the old man peered through the binoculars from his hotel room in downtown Gulfport. Living in hotel suites was his way, liking the independence of fewer domestic chores, and Mazie went along with this arrangement as her health was failing.

A ship on the horizon caught his eye as well as a few sailboats just clearing the ship channel, moving more quickly across his view. Then, appeared a sudden movement below, nearer the hotel—a brief flash and then gone.

He put down his glasses and reached for the Dutchmaster cigar, sitting like a brown turd on the edge of the heavy glass ashtray, and took a deep draw, allowing the smoke to billow about his head. He was a lawyer of the old school, in his veins for generations through the Neville branch that emigrated from Scotland years before the Revolutionary War. A retired Chancery Court judge, he was a well-known character on the coast from Pass Christian to Ocean Springs, both in and out of the courtroom, at home, and in New Orleans and Mobile.

Reaching for the glasses, he peered at the corner where the flash occurred, unsure of what he saw. Acuity wasn't what it had been these last few months since those two dizzy spells. Nothing there now and the building corner was only a scant block away. Curiosity piqued, wanting to explore, hesitation entered, as it was July. The afternoon was humid and heavy with anticipation of a subtropical shower, while the lazy hum of the ceiling fan invited immobility.

What the hell? he thought. Taking his straw hat and black

umbrella, he stepped into the hall and moved down the passageway to the elevator, punching the call button. Stepping in, he mumbled, "Sure do miss a chat with Oscar. Damn automation." Oscar, the black elevator operator, had been replaced a year before.

Out onto the slick marble floor of the Art Deco lobby, he clambered down the steps to the revolving entrance door. *Damn Mazie, this umbrella isn't necessary. Oh hell, peace in the house is a blessing. I'll call Oscar, he's a wise man, and I sure miss him. A chat will do us both good.*

The wall of humid heat met him as he ventured forth, a spry man who belied his age of 85, in his white linen suit, straw hat, and spectator shoes.

Although his career kept him primarily indoors—the court, his office, and libraries—he kept physically fit from a lifelong obsession with fishing and, until the past ten years, dove and quail hunting.

The only person on the street was a young man with an armload of what appeared to be files, headed for the law offices across the street. Looking both ways, the judge proceeded toward the corner a block away, appearing to be moseying along with a slight shuffle; however, he was acutely scanning every item of debris on the sidewalk and in the gutter. As he approached the corner, he noted a small greasy smudge on a building about five feet above the sidewalk, on the corner, with a small stain beneath.

"What the hell is this?" he exclaimed. Leaning over, he sniffed deeply. "What is this odor? It's unfamiliar but it has a familiar key. Where have I smelled this in the past? Somewhere, I recognize something, but what, where, who wore this scent? Damn my memory, I need to relax to bring it back." He whispered under his breath.

He then noticed a crumpled card on the sidewalk. Picking it up, he read *Notti's, where more is not enough*, with a Biloxi exchange phone number. Familiar with every establishment on the coast, having lived there for over fifty years, he had no knowledge of a Notti's. It was a tonic taken; a spring came to his step and mind. Looking about, seeing nothing on the street for several blocks and only a pickup truck passing, he quickly retreated to his hotel room to deliberate further.

❖

TWO

At the local mental health clinic, murmuring voices penetrated the wall of Trish McLeod's office.

"He's so bad Percy, mumble, mumble," whined a female voice. The soundproofing was poor in the clinic, built in the sixties, and Trish was continually vexed at listening to Percy and his clients, especially since his therapy skills were so poor. Many of the times when she heard more clearly she wanted to scream, "Let her talk," but that wasn't the way in this system. Comments regarding therapy were not welcome from university professors, especially to social workers with thirty years experience.

Then the voices became louder and louder. "I've had it!" said Mary Lou, Percy's client (his were clients, hers patients) and then the slam of the door to the hall. Again the sound of a door opening came through the wall.

Maybe I'll have some peace now, she thought, hearing the squeak of the door to the women's toilet across the hall.

"Why can't that damn maintenance man use a little oil?" she exclaimed under her breath. "Boy, am I crabby today. Must be my PMS. Damn all men anyway. They can use oil when they want to, if they think it will get them a piece of tail." She was off on one of her internal dialogues when a loud, shrill shriek and the screech of the toilet door broke the silence.

Trish opened her door and stuck her head out. "What's up?"

Mary Lou bolted from the restroom her face blanched and in a rasping voice screamed, "There's a body in the tub!"

By this time, Percy was in the hall, his long, curly hair pulled back in a ponytail, incongruent with the official dress code of tie and slacks.

Mary Lou cried, "I'm never going to pee in that room again!"

"Would you check Dr. Trish?" asked Percy.

"Sure."

She entered the three-stall toilet, which contained a large porcelain tub left over from initial construction, never used, with marble walls and a grab bar.

"Oh my God! Holy shit!"

Her hand went to her mouth.

The body was askew in the tub. Blood splattered the walls, and dripped in a thick pool under the limp fingers draped over the side of the tub, the head held extended in place by hair tangled on the faucet. A horizontal slash had taken the jugular, external carotid artery, and trachea in one stroke.

Trish backed out into the hall, her hand still over her mouth. "Call Clyde. It's real!"

Clyde, the off-duty policeman who was security for the day, sauntered up. "What's up?"

Trish was sure Clyde never dreamed he would have a homicide to report to that Detective Bill Swanson, whom he not so secretly called B.S., and who was always on his case.

Clyde, opening the door said, "You guys trying to put one over on me? Percy, you're always the joker."

"Not this time, bud. This is for real and gory. Hold on to your guts if what I glimpsed is accurate."

Two steps into the toilet, "You women are always—" he stopped mid-sentence as the corpse came into view. "Whoa," he said with a gulp that verged on a gasp. "Let me call Central Office and get some detectives out here. Percy, tell staff to secure all patients currently on the second floor in the waiting room, and instruct staff to wait inside their offices with the doors shut until okayed to leave by the team."

Trish re-entered her office. Inside, she sat on the blue

vinyl sofa instead of the desk chair and closed her eyes. The gory scene overcame her, so she opened her eyes. *Did I go in that toilet this morning? Sure, I arrived at the office shortly after 8:00, put my purse in the right-hand, bottom desk drawer, then I closed the drawer, opened my lunch tote, took out my soy drink, and wolfed it down without enjoying it. I called the desk, and asked if my 8:30 had checked in yet? Shanella said no but she'd let me know.*

At 8:45 I used the toilet. The soy drink is like clockwork, always 30-35 minutes later I have to pee. The blue stuff was in the toilet. I used stall #3 because stall #2 and #1 leak sometimes, so I think I was the first to flush it this morning.

As she ran her thoughts through her mind, the horror of the body came again to the foreground. She'd only had a glimpse. The woman was white, with dirty-dishwater blonde hair. *Hell where did that come from?* She hadn't seen dirty dishwater in 30 years. The throat wound gaped open and the white exposed cartilage of the trachea was worse than the blood. She became aware she was trembling.

Shut up mind, cut this out! I didn't even look at her face to see if I knew her. Oh God! Think of something else not the gore.

She was dressed a step above what most patients and staff wore, linen slacks, Ferragamo sandals, and batiste shell under a big shirt jacket, all in a pale robin's egg blue.

Can't you turn your damn mind off? This is useless. She chastised herself only to have the image of the corpse roar forward again a moment later with the stark contrast of dark wine, red blood, on robin's egg blue linen in the foreground.

"If I don't close it down I think I'm going to puke," she whispered.

Feeling the bitter acid bile of the partially digested soy drink rise in her throat and saliva pool in her mouth, she swallowed several times, breathed deeply, and avoided retching. Next, she picked up the phone and punched in Barb's number at the medical center. Barb, her best friend (they had adopted each other as sisters when both found they had such similar interests), was a toxicologist who did at times forensic work as a consultant on criminal cases.

For once the voice mail didn't come on, and it was a refreshing balm to hear Barb's slightly Yankee voice say, "Hello?"

"Barb?" Trish clutched the receiver. Her fingers blanched. "What's wrong?"

"How do you know something is wrong?"

"I can tell by your voice. You're breathing heavily, and I hear a crack in your voice."

They were so close that sometimes it seemed they read each other's minds.

"I'm at the mental health clinic today."

"I can tell. It's on the readout on my phone."

"Oh, I forgot you have that. Oh, Barb, we just found a bloody corpse in the old bathtub in the bathroom across the hall from my office."

"Jesus, a corpse? In a tub at the clinic? Did you find it?"

"No, a patient from the next office went in, and then Percy asked me to check as she was hysterical and… Oh, Barb, it's so awful, so bloody—her throat is slit—the trachea is exposed!

It's worse than work in the morgue as med student, because it happened ten feet across the hall—so close. I was just in there this morning and didn't look back there. Sometimes I do. I was peeing right beside this!"

"Hold on, you're okay. Do you want me to come out?"

As she heard Barb's words of reassurance, Trish felt hot, wet tears well up and flow out of her squeezed eyelids.

"I wish you could, but we're all quarantined in our offices, and I'm sure they won't even let you in the building. I'll call you tonight."

A few minutes later there was a knock at the door, and she jumped up to open it. A policeman in a navy sport coat, khaki slacks and yellow tie, looking very Ivy League, stood in the doorway.

"Dr. McLeod?"

"Please. Dr. Trish; all the psychiatrists at the center are called 'doctor and first name' by patients and staff alike. It's more friendly."

"May I come in? I'm Detective Swanson."

"Sure, have a seat."

"You saw the body?"

"Yes, Percy asked me to check."

"Had you been in there earlier today?"

"Yes, about 8:45."

"Did you notice anything strange?"

"No, I went to the third stall, from habit, and noticed blue toilet bowl cleaner in the other bowls. I remember thinking I was the first person to come in this morning. Now that I think about it, there was an unusual odor."

"Odor?"

"Yes, I wasn't sure what it was, something different, but in some way a little familiar. I don't think it was perfume, but more like the trash hadn't been emptied and something from yesterday was left there, hand cleaner or mouthwash or special soap or…I don't know, something strange. Cloying. It was more than the usual odor in a women's toilet."

"Did you notice anything else out of the ordinary?" He pressed her.

Trish frowned as she spoke. "As I was washing my hands I noticed all the mint/fruit flavored condoms were gone from the large supply kept in a container attached to the back of the door. And they had been there yesterday the last time I used the toilet."

"What time does this place close?"

"On that day it stayed open until 5:30, but I left at 4:30. Only a few staff man the clinic until 5:30." At this point Trish began to wonder where the questioning was leading. "Officer, I'm shaken. How much more do you need? I'd like to leave now."

"I guess this will be all for now. Could you come by headquarters to have your fingerprints taken?"

"Sure, no problem."

Trish took her purse, leather briefcase, tote bag of catalogues, and golf umbrella then locked her desk and office door, and stopped by the reception desk to say she was leaving. Yellow police tape required her to navigate the long way around to the elevators; however, she was glad to avoid the door to the toilet.

Downstairs, the patients had all left and those not yet seen, rescheduled. Popping the umbrella for the short, hot humid walk to the parking lot, she approached her dirty Ford Explorer.

She backed out of the slot that was her favorite, always in the shade after 2 p.m., but today that didn't help. She headed west on the I-10 toward the medical center, not knowing what fires were there to be put out or at least contained. Trish set the cruise control. *The last thing I need is a speeding ticket now.*

She once again went over the scene in the toilet. *The blood was dark, almost black, so I know it had been at least four or five hours since death. Blood was everywhere, but there was something strange about the spatter pattern. Maybe she bled without a struggle, just spurted from arteries.*

I didn't touch her so I don't know if she was stiff or not. And then there was that funny smell, and why were all the mint/ fruit-flavored condoms gone?

Her thoughts slowed as she entered the parking garage with her access card and found a spot near the elevators and walkway to the medical school.

She was sweaty as she made her way to her office on the third floor where she unlocked the door, turned on the light and computer, then plopped into the desk chair. She pulled open the top right drawer and reached way to the back, retrieving a clean pair of panty hose and a can of talc powder. Shucking her shoes, she hiked her skirt and pulled off the sweaty panty hose, then dusted liberally with the talc from crotch to toes. *Sometimes, small pleasures are the best.* She felt refreshed. Picking up the phone she dialed her secretary.

"Is he in today?"

Sheila, who knew she was asking about the chief, replied, "No, he's in Crete."

"Crete? You mean they have medical meetings there?" said Trish as she rolled her eyes.

"I guess so. We're not supposed to know. He left last night, and Cindy was in a twit to get the reservations completed. It was a real rush job."

"Great, at least a little peace for a week or so! Any calls I need to take?"

"Yes, call Dr. Barb as soon as you can, and a fellow by the name of Neville called. Said he was a retired Chancery Court judge and needed to talk to you."

"Talk to me or make an appointment?"

"He said 'talk to you.' He had observed something or found something and wanted to discuss it with you."

"Okay, I'll call him. He was a friend of Great-Uncle Wallace, so it must be important. I'm surprised the old goat doesn't have his tail in a crack over something again. I thought he was getting too old for that."

Scribbling the number, she said, "I know you don't usually do this, but could you bring my mail in to me? I need to talk to you about something."

Sheila pulled the pile of junk mail and a few first class envelopes from Dr. Trish's box and scurried down the hall, transferring her calls to Kennetta the clerk, first.

"What's up, Doc?" she said as she entered Trish's office. "You always remind me of Bugs Bunny when you say that, maybe it's your carrot red hair!" teased Trish as she smiled at Sheila.

Sheila relaxed a bit. "What have I done now?"

"You're too sensitive, Sheila. You do excellent work. I have no complaints."

"Well, it's just that you're about the only faculty member who treats me like I'm a real human being, who has a life and feelings."

"Sorry but I can't cure the world for you, Sheila. All that aside, I need to talk to you, seriously. Did you hear what happened at the mental health clinic today?"

"The murder?"

"God, word travels faster than the speed of light around here, and its approaching warp speed. Yes, did you know I saw the body?"

"No! Jesus help me, it must have been awful."

"It was. What I need from you is strict silence. Do not say anything to anyone about me. Simply say, 'You'll have to ask her yourself,' and I'll handle it. Got it?"

"Got it!"

"Great." Trish then punched in the Gulfport exchange number and dismissed Sheila with a smile and a nod of her head.

"Judge Neville's suite, please?" The old aristocrat liked his calls to come through the switchboard, even though they could be sent directly to his room.

Why do they still call him 'Judge?' At least it beat 'Your Honor.' Wonder if those stories of how he entertained Tulane law students with his ribald humor in the French Quarter were true?

Probably so, from what Trish had known of the old fellow.

She heard him called a brilliant, persistent bastard, but of the utmost fairness and reverence of the law; a great judge and in his early years, a relentless defense lawyer.

The phone switched to elevator music, and in a moment, a deep, sonorous baritone voice with a southern accent, thick as molasses in January, came on. "Henry Neville speaking."

"Judge? This is Trish returning your call."

"Oh, thank you, my dear, so kind of you. Would you give me the pleasure of coffee, spiked with a little brandy, if you like, in the next few days at Bonnie Jean's?"

She really felt not in a mood to meet with an old family friend, but family was important, so she said "How about Saturday, 10 a.m.?"

"Fine, I'll be there," replied the Judge as he puffed and stroked his cigar.

"How's my Mazie?"

"Fair to middling and holding on. So kind of you to ask."

"See you then, 10 a.m. Saturday. Good-bye."

"Good-bye, my dear," and the line was silent.

Trish smiled to herself. *What is that old goat up to? He is brilliant and has such a curious mind that at the least it will be a pleasant diversion from the events of this day.*

The mail, consisting of a stack of throwaway junk mail, a couple of journals set aside to read later, and several subscription renewals, was her first task.

That finished, the e-mail needed to be checked. What seemed like fifty or so were deleted after reading. *Thank goodness only a few require a reply.*

At five Trish packed up her ancient Hartman, a gift from Aunt Jeanie upon graduation from medical school, hiked her purse over her shoulder, and carefully locked her desk, turning off the computer, the light, and closing the door. She stopped by the break room fridge for a cold bottle of water for the hot trip home. She scurried down the hall to the parking garage exit. Even in the parking garage, the heat was oppressive, a wall of humidity.

At least the A/C will kick in quicker since it's shaded, she thought, as she opened the door and tossed her briefcase and purse to the passenger side of the front seat and inserted the cold water in the holder. Seconds later she snapped it open taking a swig as she started the engine. The garage was nearly empty and creepy, even at this hour. Most staff, students, and faculty left at 4:30, and only hospital staff cars remained.

Easing out of the garage, she edged onto the interstate heading east to her exit several miles away. Traffic was relatively light in this direction. The sun was still hot, but as she glanced south, there was a bank of clouds out over the Gulf that looked promising. It was hurricane season anyway. This year so far there had not been any activity in the Gulf. There had not been a major Category 5 since Camille many years before, only a few near misses, and two years ago George was only a Category 1.

Some tropical showers would be nice. I'll have to water the yard if it doesn't rain soon.

❃

THREE

She took her exit and drove down the street into a subdivision of single-family homes. Pulling into the drive, she hit the garage door opener and parked in the center of the double space.

This is great, she thought closing the door.

Since her divorce from Larry two years before, she allowed herself this luxury of not being cramped. As she opened the door to the laundry room, the fragrant odor of garlic greeted her, as well as Smoke, her blue point Siamese, who mewed a greeting.

At least I do some things well, she thought.

A chicken breast had simmered in the slow cooker, joined by a rich herbal broth of tomatoes, celery, bell peppers, and onion. All she needed was a quick spinach leaf salad and a glass of wine. As she pulled out the bag of spinach, Skip, her 'pound puppy,' scratched at the sliding patio door, whining for entry, tail wagging vigorously.

"Okay, sweetie," she said as she opened the door.

She couldn't decide which she loved more, Skip or Smoke. Each was dear in his special way. Skip was part golden retriever and black lab and God knew what else. Not as large as a purebred, he had the retriever personality, was loyal, and was always ready to play or go for a walk. He and Smoke got along well, when Trish remembered to give Smoke's claws a weekly manicure. Even though he was a house cat, she couldn't bear to have him declawed, as most of her friends had done with their cats. It was enough to have him neutered.

Skip wagged his tail vigorously as she rubbed him about his ears and knelt to give him a hug. "Good boy!" Smoke wound around her legs begging for his share of attention.

She walked through the orderly house to her bedroom, where she kicked off her shoes and fell back on the king-sized bed. It was great to have Mercedes, her housekeeper, come in twice a week and keep things tidy.

Trish sat up and surveyed her bedroom, an oasis for her. Although the ceiling fan wasn't necessary, it gave a tropical note to the room. To the right was the master bath with a large oval tub that overlooked a small walled garden of tropical plants, elephant ears, bamboo, and hanging baskets of Tahitian wedding flowers.

Opposite the bed was a large entertainment center. Behind doors of fruitwood cabinetry, Bose speakers flanked the TV, VCR, and DVD player. A small assortment of videos, mostly her favorites—James Bond, Hornblower, and a few Star Treks from the original series—filled a shelf. Her CDs were varied—Chopin, Beethoven, Vivaldi, Bach, Tibetan Chants, Paul Horn, and Nat King Cole.

She took a pair of baggy seersucker shorts and tee tank off the closet shelf, slipped thongs on her feet, and headed for the kitchen.

She poured herself a glass of wine and filled a chili bowl with the chicken-garlic-tomato stew. She sat down with Skip at her side, waiting expectantly, watching every movement.

As she sipped the wine and began dinner, her mind drifted back to the events at the mental health clinic that morning. She did not go to the clinic every day, but this week she had been there one afternoon, yesterday, and the following morning, today. Medical students had been seeing patients for their psych rotation yesterday afternoon and she had stayed until the last of their patients were seen and the student notes reviewed and signed.

She proceeded with the meal, saying out loud to Skip, "Who says you can't eat stew in the summer?" Skip wagged his tail and lifted one paw. "I wish I had never taught you that trick," she said handing him a morsel of chicken.

She thought back to the body. *Now I wish I had looked longer. She was dressed in linen. Not many, if any, of our patients can afford linen, and she had manicured nails with red nail polish. I didn't notice any jewelry. God! That was awful the way her hair was tangled and caught on the faucet, pulling her throat open to expose the trachea.*

Trish stopped eating as she remembered the strange smell.

"What could that have been, Skip?"

Skip thumped his tail again in expectation. This time, no food was forthcoming however, as his mistress continued eating.

Trish finished her meal and turned on the six o'clock news to hear the report of the death at the mental health clinic.

"Authorities are not giving any details as the investigation is still under way. However, they have announced that the victim is Hilda Rasberry, a prominent figure in the community and a master gardener. There are no further details at this time."

That's strange, thought Trish, *they didn't even say how she was killed. What was a person like Hilda Rasberry doing at a mental health clinic?*

Trish racked her memory. Had she ever met Hilda? She didn't think so, even though she was somewhat interested in gardening and frequented the plant nurseries for ideas.

Just then the phone rang. Checking it, she recognized her mother's number.

"Darling, don't you go to that mental health clinic sometimes?" her mother began.

"Yes, Mama, I do."

"Were you there today?"

"Yes, Mama."

"I just heard this terrible report about Hilda Rasberry being murdered there. Did you see her?"

"Well, to tell the truth, I did. Her body was in the restroom just across the hall from my office."

"I told you never to go to medical school. You could have had a nice career teaching in a college somewhere."

"Now, Mama, let's not get into that again. That was over twenty years ago. You didn't know her, did you?"

"Come to think of it, I saw her at the Garden Club before I stopped going a few years ago. She was always so sweet and cheerful, never a harsh word. I can't imagine why anyone would want to kill her."

"Well, someone evidently didn't think she was 'sweet and cheerful' and they killed her. How's Pops?"

"Oh, just fine. By the way, did Judge Neville call you? I gave him your number at the medical center."

"Yes, he did. I'm meeting him for coffee at Bonnie Jean's Saturday morning."

"Give him our best, and tell him we want Mazie and him to come for some homemade ice cream soon. I'll call Mazie. She's always been such fun. Even now, with her health failing, she's a delight. Sometimes, I wonder how she's put up with him all these years."

"I'll consider an invitation, too, if you don't use heavy cream."

"What's ice cream if you don't use heavy cream?" her Mama said. "All right, Half and Half and Junket for you. Bye, now. Love you."

A rumble of thunder sounded through the house, and the late afternoon darkened with the approach of a thunder-shower from the southwest. The patter of rain on the patio was simultaneous with Skip's vigorous scratching at the bottom of the door having finished his supper outside..

Letting the eager dog in, damp with raindrops, Trish took a chair in view of the now quite heavy downpour and picked up the phone to call Clyde. Ordinarily, she wouldn't have the home phone number of one of the off-duty policemen who moonlighted at the clinic, but his wife, Susie, baked the best cakes on the coast. Trish's mother bought special ones from her, so Clyde was a contact.

Clyde answered the phone in a higher tone, southern voice than his hulk of a body would indicate.

"Dr. Trish here, Clyde. Got a minute?"

"Sure, Dr. Trish."

"Well, I'm upset about the events at the clinic this morning, and there was very little on the TV tonight. I wondered if you could tell me anything more?"

"I'm not on the inside in cases like this, so all I hear is by word of mouth. That prick Detective B.S.! Sorry, Dr. Trish, the language. It's just…he's always on my case every time I come in contact with him, and I do a good job."

"I know, Clyde."

Trish turned off the TV, picked up her emery board, and began filing her nails cocking the phone on her ear.

"It looks like the body had been there several hours. We won't know until they do the post, but she was killed well before the clinic opened this morning."

Fear grabbed her throat as she remembered her visit to the restroom that morning just after arriving at the clinic. *How could I have not noticed anything, not glanced at the tub as I sometimes do?*

"I only took a glance. It looked like her head was held up and back by her hair tangled in the faucet."

"Yep, you're right. That faucet is up higher on the wall than your usual one, and the tub is oversized compared to what's seen today. Big enough to bath four younguns at once."

"So do you think she was killed in there?"

"Since there was no blood outside the immediate area of the tub, 'pears so."

"Could she have been unconscious and placed in there before her throat was slashed?"

"Looks that way to me. No sign of a struggle. Of course, we'll have to see what McInnis says."

McInnis was the county coroner, an expert forensic

pathologist to boot, who ran a tight ship and was highly respected across the country—wouldn't let anything slip by. Trish had been called in several times by his office for consultations, even though she wasn't a forensic psychiatrist.

"I jist get the feeling she was brought in sometime during the night after the cleaning crew left, dumped, and then her throat slit," Clyde added.

"What about the security locks?" Trish asked. "Aren't they monitored?"

"Supposed to be. Also, the cleaning crew is supposed to reset them when they leave."

The State had finally come up with an alarm system a few years earlier, after several break-ins at the clinic. Only four or five people had a key to the building, outside of the cleaning crew. The alarm key had to be turned off within fifteen seconds or all hell broke loose, and a signal went off at Bayou Security, who then called the police.

Clyde said, "I suppose that could be overridden. I'm not sure they can tell at Bayou Security if someone resets the alarm. Maybe only if it goes off first."

"Do you have a key?"

"Nope, only the manager and supervisors of each unit and some contractors have one, as far as I know."

The clinic, although near the freeway, was in a light industrial area that was deserted after office hours. It sat on a large lot—three to four acres—and abutted on a wide, frequently overgrown, and snake-filled drainage ditch across the back and one side with a low income, single-family subdivision on the other. A cyclone chain-link fence wound along part of the ditch. This marked an area where portable buildings had stood many years before when some high-risk, behaviorally disordered kids attended school on the grounds. Kids from the subdivision skated on the parking lot. The clinic was built on a slightly elevated area, and any semblance of height was welcome for skateboarders, as hills were slight and few.

Clyde continued, "That's about all I know. Please don't tell

Detective Swanson I talked to you. Know any more about the victim?"

"My mama thinks she knew her slightly from the Garden Club. How was she identified?"

"Well, there wasn't a purse or anything. She had a receipt in her pocket from Lowe's for some potting soil and granulated fertilizer, so that's how they found out her name so quick."

"Do you think McInnis will do the post tonight? She's pretty high profile in some segments of the community."

"Probably not. He likes to work in the morning and, per usual, it will be a few days before he gets a report out."

"Well, thanks, Clyde. My best to your wife. Her cakes are the best. In the better than sex category."

"I'm not too sure about that, but they are good. Thanks, and I'll tell her. Bye now. Ya'll take care."

❁

FOUR

The rain had ceased and was now dripping. The sun streamed through broken clouds, still somewhat low in the trees. A nice sunset for somebody, thought Trish, but not me. The tall pines across the property line prevented such a view from her house.

She turned on the music center, shuffling the CD stack until the soothing piano sounds of Chopin flowed from the large speakers. She turned down the volume, took the last sip of wine, and went into the bathroom, turning on the tub water. Larry, her ex, had hated Chopin, preferring Rock all the time with some occasional Rap. She rolled her eyes involuntarily at the thought. Bath time was a ritual she savored. Adding bubble bath and 'Skin-So-Soft,' she shed her clothes for a soak.

"Damn those dermatologists!" Hers had informed her recently that baths should only be twenty minutes max, because her skin was drying out.

"I'm only forty-two!" she'd wailed at Ron her former classmate and now her dermatologist. She still considered herself to be a lithe, athletic woman with the build of a swimmer. She had swum in college and taught swimming in the summers at Gulf Shores Girls Camp.

"Follow my instructions and you'll keep your good skin, and don't forget to wear white cotton gloves when you drive."

"Do you tell all your patients that?"

"Yes, I do, especially when they're over forty and have fair skin."

As she stepped in the tub sinking down into the freesia scented bubbles, Trish wondered if Hilda's skin had been fair or if she had worn cotton gloves when she drove.

Smoke took his usual position on the edge of the tub. Since kittenhood, he'd been fascinated with the bubbles, as well as an empty tub. He gingerly pawed at the bubbly foam.

"One of these days, you're going to get a shock, jumping into what you think is an empty tub," she said out loud.

Glancing across the bath, she noted the time on the digital clock on the vanity. "Got to be good and follow orders!" she told Smoke. "Only twenty minutes and you can have your play tub back."

Being good and following orders was part of what resulted in the marriage to Larry, who turned out to be a real loser. Now, she felt sorry for him, but any spark of passion was long gone, and was now only a pile of cold gray ashes in the corner of her heart. At one time, when she was fresh out of medical school, the tall, handsome engineer who worked at Ingalls, the shipyard over at Pascagoula, had been exciting and her mama had insisted he was a good catch. Following parental and church rules, she refused to live with him until after the wedding. Now, she thought that had been a mistake of the first order.

Her twenty minutes up, she flipped the drain and stepped out of the tub. She carefully patted her skin with a thick towel. "Don't rub," she said to Smoke, who was waiting for the water to drain from the tub. That was another order from Ron.

"Guess I'll put on my jammies," she said to Skip. "Who says a person can't talk to her animals or to herself. My patients do it all the time."

Trish ran a very active self-talk and, for the most part, was internal with it, but at home, with her animal friends/children, she spoke out loud. They seemed to like it. In anticipation, Skip jumped on her bed and curled up at the foot, and Smoke waited for her to pull back the spread before going to his place in the center of the bed.

"Hey, I'm in charge here and get first choice," she said, gently moving him aside. The cat protested with his raspy Siamese voice.

Trish pulled a book from her bedside stack. By habit she read three or four books at a time, which most of her friends, and especially Larry, thought crazy. Barb number two—Trish had several Barb friends and had to start adding a number to their names to keep them straight—who did the same thing, understood.

"How about Steven King?" she said out loud to Smoke. "He has such access to primary process material. I need to get into Psychotic City. Reality City is too much at this time."

She immersed herself in the book for an hour and then remembered, "Skip, I forgot to take my calcium. Yes, must be good and follow the rules."

She padded into the kitchen where vitamins and assorted old medicine bottles were stored, saying out loud, "At least they have these chocolate-flavored, chewy things that taste like candy." After a glass of filtered water from the fridge, weariness descended upon her. She crawled under the covers, thinking, *I need to get a doggy door*, as she dropped quickly into a deep sleep.

Around 1:30 a.m., she was awakened by Skip whining, no barking. "If you go out now, you are out for the remainder."

Skip waved his tail as she let him out the patio door, locking it securely after him. Returning to bed, it took a little longer for her to go back to sleep as her thoughts wandered to Larry. *Maybe if I'd had a child, things would have been better. No, I'm sure that was a good decision. I wasn't ready for motherhood then.* Her nieces and nephew, children of her brother, Sam, were a delight, but for now she would practice motherhood skills on Smoke and Skip.

She drifted back into a deep sleep, to be awakened by the alarm at 6:30. The Lord's Prayer immediately flowed through her mind. She didn't consider herself particularly religious, yet it had happened most mornings since a college retreat with the Westminster group. *Maybe it's protective,* she thought.

❈

FIVE

Not questioning her involuntary prayer, she rolled out of bed and into her morning routine, glad she wasn't in a large city facing a long commute. Cheerios and bananas with skim milk and Mate' Herbal tea followed. She had stopped caffeine, for the most part, after residency.

What to wear? The Ferragamo sandals for sure and no panty hose today. Selecting a loose, gauze crinkled rayon in a bright fuchsia and turquoise, she slipped the below-calf dress over her slender body. *I need some color to keep my spirits up today.* Actually, bright colors were terrific on her. She knew that from the compliments she usually received, something about her skin tone and brunette hair.

Checking her purse for her beeper – she had turned it off, not being on call – she picked up her briefcase. Skip barked a soft "Woof!" from the yard.

"Oh, I forgot to feed you." Throwing her purse and briefcase into the car, she opened the large plastic garbage can and scooped up his morning meal. Hurriedly, she opened the patio door and dumped the dog food into his pan adjacent to his house that he hardly ever used and checked his dishpan of water. Closing the door, Smoke added his chorus, loudly protesting.

"Oh, you, too! Okay." Smoke's food and water were in the laundry room, as was his litter box. "Here you go. Yep, your water is okay."

Smoke had a fancy water bowl that gave continuously flowing filtered water. She had given in to it as he was always asking to drink from a stream of water at the sink. His reply was a cross between a purr and a meow. Smoke began to chow down, crunching his food as she slipped out the door to the garage.

The sun was already bright and hot, the shrubbery still glistening from the previous night's shower, even at 7:30 a.m. Traffic was light as she exited the subdivision gate, honking at Maxine, her neighbor, who was weeding her petunias, taking advantage of the early morning coolness. Maxine was the green thumb of the street.

Trish wondered if she had known Hilda. The Garden Club was popular with the master gardener group, even though they had no obligation for public service gardening as the masters did. The area was graced by several projects initiated and completed by the master gardener group.

Trish suddenly remembered, it was the master gardener group who only last spring had put in a lovely herb and flower bed, the phlox now thick with blooms around the base of the flagpole at the mental health clinic. She recalled Brian, the custodian, had bitched because it made access to the flagpole a little difficult. The gardeners had graciously placed two round stepping stones in the bed so he wouldn't have to step into the loose soil of the flowerbed. He gingerly accepted the aid, but grumbled under his breath. Trish usually spoke to Brian on her arrival at the clinic, if he was around outside.

"This place's a real antique. Something's always breaking down, and they ought to replace the whole damn air-conditioning system," Brian complained that morning.

"I heard Tillie say it would cost more than the budget had this year," Trish replied.

"She better damn well do it next year," Brian grumbled, "else you folk are going to have to bring your own buzz fans and wear shorts."

He was right about that. Although the clinic had windows that opened, it was like a tin box.

"Remember last spring when the thermostat stuck? Boy, that was something!"

"Yep," Brian said, "sure was glad for those windows that morning. It must have been 120 degrees in there when I opened up at 7:30 a.m. Monday morning. Sure were a lot of pissed off social workers with their little baby plants cooked, except that cactus in your office, Dr. Trish."

Even the glue that held the number plates in place over the doors had melted, and all the plates were on the floor.

"Just more frigging work for me. Sorry, Dr. Trish." Tillie the manager, was frequently on Brian about his mouth, especially when around the kids who came to the clinic.

"Probably ain't nothing they don't hear every day at school and on the street. Damn younguns always trying to run in the building. Gonna break their damn asses when they hit a wet spot some day on that terrazzo floor. And for God's sake, that turnaround thing at the entrance is just an invitation for trouble!"

A gate had been installed, all chrome and shining, at the entrance near the downstairs receptionist's window. It had slowed down wanderers entering the building.

"At least you don't have to sweep and wax the floors."

"I'm maintenance, not no damn janitor! 'Cept, I did have to help out with that mess yesterday afternoon, late, after the cops finally let it be cleaned up. That inspector/detective, or whatever he calls his self. Asshole, prick, full-of-himself Detective Bill Swanson told me he'd 'preciate some respect. Jist 'cause I weren't bowing and scraping, he didn't have to act so high falutin.'"

As she approached her office, everything looked normal, no yellow police tape. Clutching her belongings, she inserted the key and opened the door. *No change from yesterday.* The trash basket had even been emptied.

She opened the drawer and dropped her purse into it, removed her beeper, and clipped it at the neck of her dress, checking to see if it was on buzz. After all these years, she still jumped at the 'beep.' Entering the file room down the hall, she picked up several files in her box and stopped by her other file box at the upstairs receptionist's station to retrieve her dictated reports to correct. Not stopping to chat with any coworker, she closed her door and quickly wrote her progress notes from the day before, then proofed three evaluations.

Taking the dictated psychiatric evaluations to Allie, the assistant administrator, and replacing the files on top of the file cabinets to be refiled, she gathered her purse and briefcase and exited the building. The car was already hot, even with the windows cracked. Full air-conditioning took care of that problem before she reached the freeway to the medical center.

The medical center was an impressive building from the interstate, built some fifteen years earlier, next to an old 500-bed public hospital. It had grown through the years; a clinic building for viral diseases, women and children, and cancer treatment had been added. Now, only the emergency room and inpatient beds remained in the original hospital.

The latest addition, a seven-story parking garage next to the medical school, had opened six months ago and was a welcome relief from the rain and sun. The center was a major employer on the coast, with over 5,000 employees in the medical school, hospital, and clinics.

Sheila was at her desk as Trish passed. "Morning!"

Trish, moved to her box, taking out a few messages and walked to her office down the hall. She noticed that Sheila had a new stuffed dragon on top of the file cabinet.

Trish's office was rather small and made smaller by the oversized recliner piled high with papers and journals yet to be read. She wished an office with a window would open up; however, the last time someone left, she was only an associate professor and not high enough in the pecking order to warrant getting it.

The sound machine on her desk, with an option of ocean waves or a gentle stream, was little consolation, but she clicked it on anyway, as well as the green glass covered desk lamp that softened the glare of the fluorescent lights overhead.

The notes were mostly pesky things to deal with, like the utilization review committee meeting at 4:00.

Her desk was littered with an assortment of items — a crystal snail, a gift from her pediatric social worker friend, Carolyn, a cow-shaped creamer that held a clutch of pens and pencils, a large desk calendar turned to July, covered with doodles and notes, and with the last week of July marked out. A trip to the Colorado Rockies for a medical meeting had been a relief from the summer heat these past four years. *Better stop by travel on the way out and pick up the itinerary.*

She pulled her small personal planner from her purse, noting the confirmation number for the condo in Aspen and left it on the desktop, as well as a message from her ex, ignored but taped to the calendar. There was also a note from Barb, her seventh grade friend who had retired to homemaking.

She dialed Barb's number. "What's up, Barb number one? Trish here."

"You don't think I know your voice by this time," quipped Barb.

"Yes, I suppose so."

"What about the murder at the mental health clinic? You go there some, don't you?"

"Yes, but I don't know much of anything. I'm not even sure the murder occurred there, but it sure looks like it. Did you know her?"

Barb rattled forth. "I had a couple of chats with Hilda over the past few years. She was sweet as pie. Too sweet if you know what I mean? One of those Southern belle types. I bet every hair was in place, even when she was spreading cow manure in her immaculate little garden. Her hands were always manicured. Beats me, if she was that much of a dirt-digger like the rest of us. I think those were false fingernails she had, to look that good.

"She even had a gardener; a little Vietnamese man. How

many people do you know have a gardener? Lots of us have a yardman who cuts and trims the grass, but a gardener? Give me a break!

"But, I'll give her credit for talking the talk of a gardener. Latin species and variety names rolled off her tongue like water off a duck's back. Don't know or even care if she walked the walk too."

"Well, her fingernails didn't look too spiffy when I saw her," replied Trish, "with dried blood on them and a little pool of blood coagulated on the floor beneath her finger tips."

"Oh, how horrid! Tell me more."

"Barb, look who's talking like a belle. The first gal in our crowd to insist her name be listed 'Barb Beauregard' not 'Mrs. James Beauregard' in the league phone book."

"I'm curious, even if it is horrid. Seems I remember Hilda was from up North somewhere, way up by Tupelo."

"What else do you remember about her?" Trish pumped.

"Well, she wore good clothes, not designer, but in summer always Ferragamo sandals and linen pants, sometimes with jackets, when the rest of us were suffering in sleeveless cotton. Why would she wear linen so often? It wrinkles so. I look crumpled before I get out of the car, but Hilda didn't."

"She was rather rumpled in that bathtub yesterday."

"Oh, so you saw the body up close. I knew it! Why keep secrets like that from me?"

"Barb, I shouldn't have even said that. The police said not to talk about what we had seen. Was she married?"

"No, but I think she had been or might've been a young widow. She wore a gold wedding band on her right hand like some widows do. And her eye makeup was too heavy for my taste. Almost like a Vegas showgirl, false eyelashes and all."

"I don't think she had on eyelashes yesterday, come to think of it. I couldn't keep my eyes off that gaping wound in her neck with her trachea exposed."

"Thought you weren't supposed to tell?"

"Barb number one, you're an old friend. Just add this to

our treasure house of shared secrets from the seventh grade. Remember that time you flashed those boys in the eighth grade? Gave them a little thrill, didn't you?"

"It doesn't seem like much nowadays, all they saw was skinny eighth grade legs and white panties."

"Gotta run now, Barb number one. Get you later."

"Okay, bye. Love ya."

"Love you, too."

❈

SIX

The phone was ringing as she entered the kitchen. With Smoke winding himself around her legs, she managed to answer it just before the answering machine kicked on.

"Trish?"

"Who do you think it would be, the cat?" She knew full well Steven recognized her voice as she did his.

"Are we still on for dinner at Guido's?"

"Sure. Casual?"

"What else. I can only stand a tie on Sundays these days."

"How're you getting away with that?"

"I'm the boss, remember?" Steven was the CEO of a family insurance agency and set his own dress code. "Bye for now. Love ya."

"Love you, too." It was a Southern expression that had crept into Trish's, and most of her friends' vocabulary, the past few years. When previously it had been 'Bye now,' it was now 'Love ya.'

There might be love there someday, but now it's the platonic-friendship love, not the gusty, grunting, lustful, creamy, sexy kind.

"Okay, okay, Smoke, I'll feed you." Skip was dancing at the patio door, his tail a whirlwind propeller of joy, not daring to put his paw on the glass. A smart dog, he had learned quickly that was a big no in this house.

The air conditioning had not tripped on all day, and Trish muttered under her breath, "Sure hope you're okay," as she turned the thermostat down to 70 degrees. "Here you go,

Smoke. Deli Delight cat food, your favorite. Now let me look at the mail."

The mail was in a pile under the mail slot. Taking it to the den sofa, she snapped on the TV, placing a trash basket at her feet while she watched the early news and sorted the mail.

Her mind wandered to Steven. Is there any potential there? Maybe. *He's certainly different from ol' Larry. His hair is getting a little thin at the temples.*

Steven had green eyes and skin that darkened to a bronze tan every summer from his outdoor activities, mainly his 30-foot sloop, a C&C30 that he moored at the local yacht club.

He does have a nice body, and he always looks spiffy even with a paintbrush in his hand. The thought passed through her mind that it might be nice to have a man share her life again. Steven liked her pets and the jazz and classical music she preferred. There might be some possibility of a relationship there. Time would tell.

I'm not sure he's over his wife's death. Thank goodness, there were no children. That would definitely be a negative. I'm not ruling out a kid of my own before I'm fifty, but no stepchildren for me.

❀

SEVEN

Saturday morning broke hot, humid, and heavy. Popping her multi-vitamin and calcium like she instructed her patients to do, she drank a cup of herb tea as she expected the judge to insist on more than a cup of coffee when she met him at Bonnie Jean's. Throwing on a crinkled gauze pants outfit and sandals she applied her makeup with more care for the social encounter. A light spray of Bal a Versailles and she was ready a little early. *Might as well check the plants,* she decided.

The flower beds, profuse with low-maintenance annuals, looked happy thanks to the shower earlier in the week; however, the three large hanging ferns across the front of the house, sheltered by the slightly overhanging eaves, needed a good drink. This accomplished, she picked up her large, straw sisal tote purse, placing inside it her weekday woven leather without bothering to dump, sort, or repack into the more summery looking bag.

The streets were nearly deserted as she approached Bonnie Jean's, a quaint house turned elegant restaurant. It was a hangout for a group of the Coast legal crowd during the week because it had a small watering hole bar located in a former back bedroom, graced by an exit right to the parking lot. Pulling into the much-prized shaded parking lot, Trish selected a slot that was sure to remain in the shade at least until 11:30. Shady parking places were premium on the Coast. Even with AC it took fifteen minutes to cool down a vehicle after only an hour or so in the brutal summer sunshine. As expected,

Judge Neville's ancient Caddy already graced another shady spot.

Entering, she immediately spied him in his white linen suit, long-sleeved shirt, and stupid knit tie. The casual, comfortable room was dotted with several tables of what appeared to be fathers treating children to breakfast out. Trish suspected most were getting started on a visitation weekend of shared child custody arrangements.

"Hi, judge, how's tricks?"

"Tricks, my dear? Whatever do you mean?" His sonorous baritone voice dropped to a discreet, quiet tone as he graciously rose, pulled out her chair, and seated her. He sat down himself before signaling to the waitress that he was prepared to order.

"Nice touch," Trish said, as she smelled the fresh summer bouquet centered on the small table covered with a spotless white tablecloth, silver-plated tableware, and cloth napkins. "As much as I hope you enjoy my company, something must have piqued your insatiable curiosity for you to issue this invitation."

"Ah, my dear, how correct you are, but that can wait a moment or two until we are served. I have always thought that you have considerable curiosity yourself. Please order, my dear."

"Coffee and two biscuits, please."

"I'll have the same," said the judge. "These are the best biscuits around. Homemade. You know."

"As good as my mama's."

"By the way, how's your mother?"

"Just fine. I'm trying to get them to come to Colorado with me for a week, but Daddy is worried about the mile-high altitude. He'll adjust, I'm sure, as they both walk the beach at some ungodly hour, five times a week."

"Jelly or molasses?"

"Molasses," said Trish. "Reminds me of fall up on the farm where it's cooler than this inferno we're living in here."

"A meeting in Colorado, my dear?"

"Yes, of sorts. Lectures and discussion groups in the mornings, and afternoons free to hike, explore, bike ride, read, and people watch."

"People watch. That reminds me, Trish, of why I asked you to come."

"Still messing around with those binoculars of yours, judge?"

"Hmmph, just checking out nature. One can see many interesting birds, even from a hotel window."

"What kind of birds have you seen lately? People 'birds,' maybe? Indiscreet love birds?"

"No, nothing like that." He tossed the crumpled card to Trish. "Ever heard of this place?"

Scanning the card and looking on the back, Trish returned it, saying, "No. Is it important?"

"Recently, I observed something unusual from my window, and when I went to investigate, I found this near the spot."

"Did you call the number?"

"Of course. It rang a long time before an answering machine came on, giving no information except to leave a number, which I did. Several days passed with no reply, so I called again, and this time the number had been disconnected. In addition, there was a greasy looking smudge on the corner adjacent to where I found the card. It exuded an unusual odor I could not identify, but which seemed somewhat familiar."

"And you think there's a connection?"

"Well, I'm not sure. There might be."

"How so?"

"A few times, three to be exact, when I have been on my evening constitutional, I have come upon rather suspicious meetings between two fellows, always different, and as I approach, they stop talking, separate, and walk in opposite directions. On two occasions, one got into a car parked nearby, leaving quickly. I believe you now say 'dug out.' One looked Mexican, I am sure, and one like a 'moonie' from over at Bayou Labatre way."

"That was Korean or Vietnamese, judge."

"Oh, well. Not the usual white redneck or colored man."

"We call them 'black' now, judge."

"They are colored and will always be that to me."

The judge was rather conservative in some ways. Desegregation had never sat too well with him, but he didn't express himself out loud in general about his views.

"I think you're just a little bored and looking for some excitement. I tell you what. Come September, I'll drive you over to New Orleans, and we'll check out a couple of your old haunts in the Quarter."

"Whatever are you speaking of, my dear?"

"Don't pretend with me, judge. I've heard about your train trips and how you partied with law students after exams, while Mazie stayed home with the children."

"Ah, well, maybe a few times, to relieve the tension of being on the bench."

"Ah, were there some pretty ladies around also?"

"Wherever did you hear this?"

"Oh, quite a few years back, I happened to overhear Aunt Anna and Mama, chatting on the porch while they shelled crowder peas, and the windows were open."

"I can assure you, it was nothing serious. Letting off a little steam."

"Okay, judge. I'll take your word. The only suggestion I have is to check in the business directory. They have the street addresses listed for phone numbers, or else call the phone company and ask them, since you aren't online."

"Think I'll do that. Thank you, my dear. And now, I have taken enough of your Saturday morning. Check, please." And he insisted on paying as they exited.

"The clientele switches on Saturday from the rest of the week, doesn't it?" Remarked Trish in the parking lot.

"Too many children for my taste," said the judge. Separating, each emptied a spot for a waiting car.

✽

EIGHT

The rental car awaiting her in Grand Junction was a welcome sight. Usually there were no problems in summer with snafued reservations, as sometimes occurred during ski season.

Wish Steven would have come. The condo has three bedrooms. Steven had acted surprised when she suggested it, then appeared downcast at the mention of three bedrooms. "I can't get away at this time. We're really busy."

Wonder if something is developing between us? she mused to herself as she drove. *This is really gorgeous scenery. Hope Smoke and Skip don't get too bent out of shape with my leaving them for a week.*

Upon entering Aspen, she picked up the keys to the condo at the real estate office. "Are you alone this year?" asked the familiar office manager.

"No, my parents are joining me for a few days, later in the week, and who knows, possibly another house guest."

"Well, make yourself comfortable. Let us know if you have any problems or need anything."

"Thanks, will do."

The condo had a large balcony that overlooked a nice view of Red Mountain across the valley. *Great place to read!* Then a contralto voice singing scales wafted over the air. *Well, maybe not so great after all. I'll have to note the times she practices and make that hike time.*

One of the joys of this time of year was the annual summer music festival, with its many free recitals. Even the street musicians were better than most available elsewhere.

Directing the husky hunk of college youth to the bedroom to deposit her luggage, she tipped him five dollars. When he looked surprised, she said, "Believe me, it's worth it. I'm not ready to tackle stairs at this altitude yet."

Everything looks the same and feels the same, she thought, as she plopped on the king-sized bed.

Making a scan of the kitchen cabinets, she always found a few items previous renters left on the shelves. She jotted down a grocery list—steak, chicken breast, salad makings, specialty breads, lunch meat, a couple of bottles of white wine, one Chardonnay, one Sauvignon Blanc. Eating out was a treat for Trish, especially in Aspen; however, the university per diem was insufficient, so home cooked meals helped keep the cost within reasonable limits. She had gone way over on the condo rental, thinking, *if I'm coming this far for atmosphere and scenery, I'm not going to hole up in some crappy motel room with no windows.*

Back from the trip to Central Grocery and Market and with the groceries put away, she selected a CD from the varied selection and a book from the shelf on things to do in Aspen, poured a Diet Coke, and headed for the balcony and the view to review the book. The meeting started the next day. Having no pressing things to attend to at the moment or for the week, Trish mulled over the recent events.

No developments in the murder at the clinic. I heard from my 'spy friend' at the coroner's office. There was a massive subdural hematoma and skull fractures, indicating Hilda was transferred to the porcelain tub from elsewhere, and then her throat was slit. She was divorced, and her ex was found in Europe on a tour with his current lady friend. Also, apparently Hilda had a lot of "friends," some who were reported to be connected in a distant way to the Serrio crime family over in New Orleans. She had a garden that had more than plants, judging from her activities. She, reportedly, frequently picked up men in antique shops on

Royal Street, of all places, and obtained mementos from them. Its no surprise the lab reported she was HIV positive.

Well, well! The sweet Southern belle wasn't the picture perfect person mama spoke of meeting at *Les Petite Jardinières*. Don't think I'll tell mama until this is all over.

Apparently she was hanging with a criminal element or at least one with shady connections, as well as the closed society of the Garden Club.

Les Petite Jardinières is more exclusive and harder to join than the Junior League on the Coast. Membership is sometimes left in wills, and there's always a long waiting list, plus needing letters of recommendation from current members. This, in addition to the possibility of a blackball, made it a very exclusive group of busybody bitches.

Trish continued her internal dialog. *What kind of person commits murder?*

For a start, frequently there is intense passion. Hilda did, at times, hang with men who thought a lot of themselves and might have an excessive need to control. It could have been done in a fit of rage or premeditated. Then, there are some who see the victim as nonhuman, so if a man has treated a number of women as objects, he could be a suspect. If he keeps that hidden, it would make it harder to pick him out.

I'm pretty sure it's a 'him,' because my contact at the police department reported that Hilda was probably alive when placed in the tub, and then her throat was slashed. To cut through that much tissue with one whack and tote her to the tub would require a bit of strength, more than most women have.

I wonder how the security system at the clinic was breached. It isn't a very sophisticated system. With a little knowledge of electronics, he wouldn't have found that difficult. It isn't clear if this was planned or if it was a loss of control for a brief moment.

Frequently, killers are alexiothymic—no words for their feelings. When you ask, "How do you feel?" they invariably say "good or bad," never anything else. Everyone around them can see by the body language what they feel, and yet they don't have a clue.

Trish usually read about murders in the paper, most of which were predictable and run of the mill—angry explosions of a jealous boyfriend or wife with a history of domestic violence.

This killing appeared more planned, and why the porcelain tub at the clinic?

How many people even knew about it? Sure, the many women who had used its facilities. And the janitorial service workers, male and female who shared the work.

Why not just kill her and leave her where the subdural was inflicted? Why move her? There are a lot of unanswered questions at this point.

What if it wasn't violent passion?

What if it was one of my patients?

Possible, in a patient with auditory hallucinations, but unlikely, unless the voices were especially strong and commanding and in those cases it's usually a close relative or the patient's attorney who gets it. I don't know anything about Hilda's relatives except for her ex who was in Europe.

Purple dusk crept up the valley as the Milky Way, not usually visible from home because of the trees, emerged in a glorious expanse. Trish, finally overcome by the long day's travel, retreated to the usual bubble bath before bed, and a deep, dreamless sleep followed.

The twittering of birds through the open window woke her the next morning. The morning air was crisp and fresh, cool and bracing, as she slipped into cords, tee shirt, and cotton crew neck sweater for the short walk to the Givins Center where the conference was held. After stopping to sign up for a rafting trip and chuck wagon picnic up the mountain, she registered and chose a seat on the top row.

Looks like many of the same crowd. This must be the fifth year I've come.

Most of these psychiatrists actually talked to their patients at length and over time, differing from the 'push-a-pill' types that were becoming the norm in many places.

Trish had contemplated private practice, but after serious consideration decided on the university, primarily because several colleagues had said solo was a lonely profession.

I like to have more people contact without the concerns of boundaries so much.

The conference this year was on boundaries, always a slippery slope that invited disaster. Just one step over the edge to physical intimacy in the closeness of psychotherapy, where changes were occurring, and there could be no way back for the boundary was violated.

Better to not even visit than run the risk. I always tell the residents that a sexual relationship with your patient is like a surgeon spitting into the open belly before closing after an exploratory lap.

That was one phrase that always resulted in a wake-up call for them regarding the damage that occurred with a boundary violation.

After the morning session, Trish looped by downtown for lunch, and soaked in the cheerful ambiance—children skating here and there, playing dodge with the sprouting fountains from the grills over the sidewalks.

Flowers were everywhere, a riot of intense color and fragrance. Flourishing flora was a favorite interest for Trish, even though she didn't put much effort into it at home. Taking a seat on one of the several benches, soaking in the scene, her mind wandered to the death of poor Hilda.

Back at the condo, she picked up the clutter that had accumulated. Her parents were taking three days to drive up.

"Need to check out and break in the new Ford," her father had said.

The remainder of the week was a pleasant interlude. No 'have-tos,' not even to attend the lectures, even though she did. The one-hour time change made for sleeping late and soundly. Contrary to some of her friends, also flatlanders, Trish slept like a rock in the mountains.

❁

NINE

It was August and hot when she picked up her new green T-Bird at the airport in Mobile. The use of Steven's truck had freed her to purchase the car.

Not as much hassle and less traffic than in Nola, she thought, as she tossed the luggage in the rear seat and headed west. *Hurricane season is upon us.* Like many on the Coast, Trish tracked the storms' weather reports on her own map.

Skip and Smoke were overjoyed to see her. Skip had pulled out a few marigold plants, a little message to let her know how bored he was.

Now, who do I know well enough in the Garden Club to call on the phone?

While in Colorado, her mama had mentioned a few names as possibilities. With her clothes beside the washer and other things dumped on the bed, she looked up a number in the phone book.

"Priscilla? Trish McLeod here. Remember me? From high school?"

"Oh, yes, it's been years! See your sweet mama at Jardinières every now and then."

"You mean the Garden Club?"

"Yes, darling. Isn't that a quaint name?" Her drawl was thick as honey.

"I just returned from Colorado. The folks came up to join me, and we were talking about the death of Hilda Rasberry."

Priscilla interrupted, "Poor dear. Isn't it just awful! No one is safe anymore."

"Well, I was curious. Mama said she didn't know her well or talk to her much and said you might?"

"Oh, yes. We had talks, before and after the meetings."

"Was she well-liked? Did anyone dislike her or did you ever get the impression she had conflicts with others?"

"She was sweet to me, but I think there are several in the club who didn't like her. I overheard Joyce asking who sponsored her."

"What was she like?"

"She could always do you one better. If my marigolds were super this year, hers were fantastic. She had an extremely high opinion of herself and didn't want to listen to anything anyone else said. Every time I started to say something, she would interrupt and tell her side of things or what she had done."

"That must not have been too much fun for you?"

"Oh, I've had lots of practice with Reggie."

Reggie was her overbearing husband, whom Trish remembered immediately.

"Thanks for talking to me. You know, I happened to be at the clinic the day her body was found?"

"Yes, I heard that. Have they arrested anybody?"

"Not that I've heard."

"Well, thanks for the chat. Nice to hear from you. Wouldn't be interested in joining Les Petites Jardinières, would you? We have a vacancy now that Hilda is gone."

"Thanks, but that's not for me."

Not in a month of Sundays! She said to herself. There's a bunch of snobby backbiting old biddies if ever I saw one. At least mama has sense enough to know not to ask me to join.

I suppose Priscilla does the best she knows, and I remember in high school she never asked anyone over to spend the night or hang out at her house on the weekends. Funny, 'cause she would always accept an invitation to do the same at somebody else's house. Now, I suspect that either her mama or daddy was a big time boozer or things were rough at home. In fact, seems I remember she came to school once with a black bruise on her face and wouldn't talk about it much. Said she fell down the back porch stairs. As a kid I didn't even think to question her answer.

Her house was built on pier and beam, as many were at that time to protect them from flooding. In fact, it was a very large raised cottage and a step above our house. An elegant cut glass surround graced the front door. The tree appeared huge at Christmas with its twinkling multicolored lights as did the azalea bushes and magnolia tree in the front yard covered with tiny white lights. To be honest, I was more than a little jealous, especially when I looked at the relatively few lights at our house. Mama said it was not good to look uppity. Priscilla never once asked me inside. A couple of times I stopped by to pick up books she had borrowed, and it was "Wait here on the porch, while I run inside and get it for you." We gradually drifted apart—not really ever connecting, but still polite when our paths crossed.

Trish was certain, as soon as she hung up, Priscilla would be hot to call her little clutch of current friends.

"Ya'll will never guess who just called me—Trish McLeod! After all these years! And guess what? She was at the mental health clinic when poor Hilda's body was found, and she had the nerve to turn down an invitation to fill Hilda's spot. I would even have sponsored her; and her mama and grandmother, God rest her soul, members! Who does she think she is? We're the most sought after club, after the league, on the Gulf coast. That's those shrink types for you. She'd probably be reading our minds or hypnotizing us anyway."

Priscilla's world was rather constricted. Reggie, although successful, was an extrovert, blowhard insurance agent in his uncle's company, and always kept her under his thumb. Not that he actually ever hit her. She was always a little cautious and sure not to push him, especially when he was hitting the bottle.

"Of course, he's not an alcoholic!" she confided to her friend, Cynthia. "He's never fallen down or had a DWI." Priscilla's idea of an alcoholic was limited, also. But she struggled and 'made do,' in her own mind, with a housekeeper whom she secretly spoke of as 'our servant,' only once every other week or less.

Talks with her Baptist pastor regarding problems with Reggie and their marriage were always met with the solution, "You're not praying enough, or you aren't praying hard enough, or read your bible more." Reggie wouldn't go to church with her, and to keep up 'appearances,' she made excuses. "His back went out on him after cleaning the gutters." It never crossed Priscilla's mind that there was anything 'really' wrong with white lies, as long as someone was protected or face was saved.

Her neighbor was amazed that as much time as Priscilla spent with her flower beds, her nails were immaculate, long and painted a ravishing ruby red.

"I always wear my gloves and lots of Vaseline," she told her, "since I don't have a real gardener, as most in the club do. I wish I could convince Reggie to get me one. Seems he gets tighter with the money every year. Junior will be going away to college in a couple of years, so maybe we need it for that."

❁

TEN

The day after her chat with Trish, while weeding her periwinkles, admiring the tough pink and white blooms, Priscilla felt something in the soil. Actually, she heard a small clank.

"Has that pesky dog buried something in my yard again?"

The terrier from next door was fond of burying 'presents' and ruining a flower plant or two in the process, but this time no flower seemed harmed or dug out. She dug a little more to find a key, somewhat weathered. Rather usual, like it was a house key, or so she thought. Priscilla was fairly certain it had not been there when she had prepared the bed, planting the periwinkles some six months previously; nor the last time she weeded, a month ago.

"Better show it to Reggie. He'll know if it's important," she said under her breath.

Placing the key in the kitchen window as she entered the house, she carefully removed her breathable work gloves and washed her hands. Vaseline was wonderful while in the dirt, but felt yucky otherwise. As she washed, her mind wandered to Reggie.

Ours was a real teenage romance. He was so handsome and a football player to boot.

Priscilla had felt special, and because Reggie was on the team at Mississippi Southern, she was on the homecoming court, the highlight of her brief college career. When they married during the summer, between Reggie's junior and senior year, his folks were unhappy, but went along because she was pregnant—and then relieved when she miscarried.

I wish I had finished. Too bad. I was passing and probably could have a job now, even if part-time. Bet I would be treated better by my associates and friends if I had the degree. Seems they treat me different, look down on me when they hear I didn't finish. The next question after, "And what were or who were your people?" was "What was your major?" It was almost as important as your sorority in the social circle she had entered.

With two years, at least I was a sorority member. This helped some in Priscilla's mind.

Just then the phone rang. Priscilla fluffed her hair and smiled into the mirror above the phone.

"Smith residence, Mrs. Smithe speaking." She spoke 'Smith' as 'Smithe.' Somehow she thought this implied higher social class, a very important concept to Prissy.

"It's me. I'll be late tonight. Don't wait up." It was Reggie.

The thought drifted through her mind, *This is getting more frequent and last time I asked, he merely said 'business' and cut me off.*

"Should I save a plate for you to buzz in the microwave?"

"No, don't bother. Be sure to pick up my shirts at the cleaners."

Yes, you have money for designer shirts, but not a helper three days a week or a gardener one day a week for me, she thought.

"Okay, honey, will do. Luv ya."

"Luv you, too."

As she replaced the phone, she remembered the early years of trying to please him. This included spending hours ironing his shirts and khaki pants, only to have him frequently toss one back on the floor of the closet if it didn't meet his specifications.

Sometimes, an insurance agent has to see clients in the evening. I don't think he needs to do that, as he did in the past, since he has several agents working with him now. I wonder if he's having an affair. No! Never Reggie! But, maybe.

The thought kept bubbling up in her consciousness, like a pot of water on the verge of a boil, with an occasional bubble.

He is still good-looking, hasn't lost his hair, but sure is developing a middle age spread. No! Not an affair. Not Reggie! I don't want to think that. I'll pray harder and read the bible more. The prayer of a righteous person availed much, and I'm righteous. Of course I am!

Denial was rampant in Priscilla's internal mental life.

After lunch, Prissy ran to the nearby Winn Dixie for a few 'fixings' for supper. Returning home, she assembled a meatloaf.

It's one of the things 'I make good,' she thought. Besides this, I do make a very good pound cake from scratch. What I really need is a cook. Reggie can be so tight with money sometimes!

As she put the meatloaf in the oven, Junior emerged from his room, draping himself around the doorframe. "What's up, Mom?"

"I wish you would call me Mama, like a proper son."

"Okay, Mops!" and he grinned, reminding her of his father at the same age.

"Your daddy won't be here for supper. Says he has business."

"Seems to me a lot of his business involves something from a bottle these days."

"Now, don't you be smart. Your father's a wonderful man and takes good care of us."

"No need to argue. I won't be back from football practice until 6:30 or 7:00."

"I'll have it ready, and we'll just warm it up. I'm making your favorite, meatloaf; even put onion soup mix and oatmeal in it. There's mashed potatoes and English peas to go with it." Creative meals were definitely not Prissy's strong suit.

"Any dessert?"

"How about instant chocolate pudding?"

"Sure, whatever? Outta here! Later."

"Bye, darling."

Priscilla was proud and happy her gangly 16-year-old played football like his dad. On the junior varsity last year, he had much praise from the coach, even making several touch-downs as an end.

I sure hope he's good enough for a scholarship to college. It might even be to Mississippi Southern. Well, wherever. The way Reggie is acting about money these days, any help will be appreciated.

An hour later, while loading an armful of clothes, including the Dockers that Reggie habitually wore, in the dryer, a card dropped onto the floor.

"That's strange. Reggie is particular since that time I didn't check his pockets and paper pieces were over everything. He cleans the pockets before tossing them into the basket now."

Bending over, now she picked up a business card—Notti's, Where More Is Not Enough—with a phone number in the Biloxi exchange, in a crisp black print on heavy stock, stock that had survived the washer. Humming *Rock of Ages*, she put the card on Reggie's dresser-top valet and dismissed it from her mind.

Priscilla was not inclined to be curious, taking most things as they came, doing her best to 'be a good girl' and 'follow the rules,' believing this was all that was necessary to lead a happy, fulfilled life. Little did she suspect there were dark clouds on her personal horizon, dark as the thunderheads building up in the southwest, out over the Gulf.

ELEVEN

It's too damn hot to walk outside, Trish thought to herself, and boy do I need to exercise. That shortness of breath while hiking in Colorado wasn't all from the altitude. Thank God, at least the gym is air-conditioned and open until eight.

Pulling on shorts and a tank top, she headed for "Ladies First," a gym for women only. Most of the clientele did not want 'sweaty, stinky men around while they were glowing.' Belles did not sweat. They either perspired or better yet, glowed. Trish, called it "sweat."

The gym was small, accommodating a maximum of ten ladies, but outfitted with good equipment and never had lines waiting for a treadmill or other Cybex torture devices. In addition, there was a large floor fan, as well as ceiling fans.

I need all the help I can get! Trish thought as she selected a treadmill close to a floor fan. Straddling the belt and punching the start button, she set the incline to 4.0 and hopped on. As she increased the speed to 4 miles an hour, she settled into a semitrance state.

Her mind drifted back to Priscilla and her spouse, Reggie. Reggie was big man on campus in high school, Mr. Everything.

Of course, he hadn't amounted to much. If his uncle didn't own that insurance business, they would certainly not have the lifestyle Priscilla believed she deserved.

I always felt there was something secretive, almost sinister, about that jock. He had such a cold hardness about those ice blue eyes. *When he smiled, his mouth moved, but there was no smile from those eyes. Probably even insisted on kinky sex.*

As she increased the incline a bit, Trish was overcome by sadness for Prissy. If life was what it appeared and her instincts correct, life was terribly hard and sad for Prissy.

She probably doesn't have one real friend she can confide in about things that really concern her. I'll give her another call and invite her over to have lemonade on the patio before it starts getting dark early.

After a few minutes, Trish felt her heart rate increase and after ten minutes, she began to sweat. *I sweat! No perspiring for me. Hell! I'm even sweating behind my knees! How I hate that, but it's a sure sign a workout is in progress.*

She remarked to a fellow member on the adjacent treadmill, "Do you know Priscilla Smith?"

"Oh, yes!"

"Do you think she works out? She always looks so trim," said Trish.

"Why, yes, I think she does, over at Premier."

Probably wears a fanny flosser outfit too. Premier wasn't the gym for Trish. Most of the male jocks worked out there, and the place was always crowed with stinky, sweaty males, with a sprinkling of 'cuties' wearing skintight spandex workout clothes. Most everyone at Trish's gym wore baggy shorts and oversized tee-shirts.

Come to think of it, she might go there because it was less expensive, but how did she get around Reggie on that one? He probably wouldn't approve of her being exposed to all the looks she was sure to get from the jocks.

❈

TWELVE

Priscilla left a plate covered with plastic wrap for Reggie, just in case, and was looking at Woman's Day. Having taken a bath, put her hair in green foam rollers, and piled herself in their king-sized bed, she also watched the day's prerecorded *Young and Restless* on the VCR. She frequently recorded her favorite soaps so as not to miss a single episode.

Reggie slammed the door, coming in from the garage.

Has a full snoot tonight, she thought. *But I'm just not in the mood to put up with anything from his mouth.*

Entering the bedroom, he leaned over and kissed her on the cheek. "How's my little woman?"

Oh, God, what's he up to now?

"Fine."

"Have a nice day?"

"Sure."

"Have something to discuss with you. Let me take a shower first."

I hope it isn't him wanting to do kinky sex things.

It hadn't always been that way over the past 25 years or so. In the beginning, he was tender and sweet. Tears welled in her eyes and her throat tightened as she remembered—but lately she feared he might actually hit or hurt her.

Reggie emerged from the bath in his blue cotton P.J.'s, his beer belly peeking out, and sat on the edge of the bed. Eyes red and bleary, he started.

"Met this fellow at lunch today. I was having an oyster

po-boy at the Old Biloxi Schooner, it was crowded as usual, and he asked if he could share the table."

"You know oysters are bad for you, and I bet they were fried. You know what the doctor said about your cholesterol."

"Hell, shut up! A man has to have some pleasure in life. You sure don't want to give any at home lately!"

Priscilla swallowed and did not reply. Experience had taught her this was not the time to pursue a discussion of his health.

"Anyway, this fellow is at the medical school. Come to find out, he's a psychiatrist. Can you believe that? We had a very interesting discussion. Seems he is doing research on sexual dysfunction. Even has this gadget he puts on the pecker to see what makes it go up. Even measures it scientifically. Said he had published papers about his work.

He also said he makes movies. Well, actually, videos of various sexual practices for education purposes. Said that doctors and students needed to be 'desensitized.' I didn't know what that meant exactly and he said it was even, if things seemed strange or not comfortable, after seeing something many times a person did not react the same way."

Oh, Jesus, protect me! Priscilla thought. Where is he going with this? I've tried to be a good, submissive wife like the bible says, but there is a limit.

Priscilla felt a lump rising in her throat, and her palms became damp.

"It seems he gets volunteers, couples, to come and do stuff, so he can tape it, and he even pays them to do it. He said he never had any problems getting volunteers under 30, but over 35, and especially over 40, not many people would volunteer. We're over 40."

Priscilla was aghast! Something in her snapped. "It's the final straw! You aren't suggesting we volunteer?"

"Well, it could be fun, and we would get paid. He said $100 for 30 minutes of action, and that's not bad."

"You're asking me to be in a porno flick? Where is your

mind? Have you disconnected your brain or, rather, is there no brain, just a tool with testicles attached?"

"Now, now. Just think about it. This is helping science."

"Oh, give me a break! Helping science? Do they do it at the medical school?"

"Well, no. He said the studio was over by Pass Christian."

"What makes you think this guy really is doing research and is a shrink at the medical school?"

"Look, he had an ID badge on with his picture and it said 'Dr. Atwater, Assistant Professor,'and 'Psychiatry' under that."

"I can't believe it! That's just not possible!" She snapped off the light and VCR, turned on her side, close to the edge of the bed. Reggie flopped on the opposite side, dropping into a deep sleep almost immediately, snoring loudly.

Priscilla's mind was racing. *Oh, God! What is going to happen to me? She prayed fervently. Protect me; let me be your servant. This can't be right! Her mind then went to Trish. Isn't she a psychiatrist at the medical school? Yes, she is, and she was nice when she called, asking about poor Hilda. Trish would know if someone was actually doing something like that. I'll call her tomorrow.*

After a considerable time, Priscilla drifted into a restless sleep.

The next morning, Reggie left the house before she awoke, unrefreshed.

In the kitchen, Junior sauntered in for his usual bowl of Wheaties, and said, "Mama, I need to get new clothes. School starts next week."

"Oh, sure, hon. We'll go tomorrow and have lunch at the mall."

"Well, maybe not lunch. I really don't want to be seen having lunch with my mom."

"Whatever," she said as she flipped open the morning local paper and scanned the pages. Suddenly she remembered what Reggie had said last night.

"Oh, Jesus!" She reached for the phone book, looking up

the Department of Psychiatry at the medical school. She took a red pen from the assortment by the phone and made the call.

"Department of Psychiatry, Sheila speaking."

"May I speak to Dr. McLeod, please?"

"Is this personal or for an appointment?"

"Personal. I'm an old acquaintance."

"She's not available at the moment. May I take a message?"

"Would you have her call Priscilla Smithe at 555-3456?"

"Be glad to. Bye now. Have a nice day."

"You too."

As she hung up, Priscilla thought, *if it's really true, Trish will know."*

It was close to 5 p.m when Trish checked her messages. Sheila was very good about beeping her if one appeared to need her immediate attention. She shuffled through the small stack, crumpling and tossing a couple from pesky drug reps.

The bane of my existence, except for ol' Jim who always has a good joke to tell. One from Priscilla. How interesting, in light of the fact I was considering calling her back.

What's she up to? She didn't call me in twenty years. Hope she doesn't want free therapy, although she probably needs it, living with that asshole, Reggie.

Trish quickly dialed the number.

"Smithe residence. Lady of the house, Priscilla, speaking."

Give me a break! I didn't know anyone talked that way these days.

"Trish McLeod here. Got your message. Sorry to be so late returning your call."

"Oh, Trish! I'm so glad you called. I can't talk now. Reggie just came home, and I'm in the middle of fixing supper. Could we get together for a chat soon? I have something I need to ask you about."

"Sure thing. I was just thinking about you the other day, after I called to see if you knew Hilda, and wanted us to get together. How about some evening, early?"

"I don't think I could manage that. Reggie is usually home then."

"Well, Sunday afternoons are good for me. Could you make that?"

"Sure, Trish. About 3:30?" *By that time, Reggie will be asleep from his 12-pack of beer.* What's your address?"

"It's 550 Bluff Creek Road off Marsh Lane third house on the right."

"I'll see you then. Have a nice evening." Priscilla continued opening the can of lima beans.

"You too. Bye now."

I wonder what's up with her?

❁

THIRTEEN

"How's the cutest, sexiest member of the psychiatry department this afternoon?" Phillip Atwater was a relatively new member of the department.

And a real slime ball, a dirt bag, Trish thought. Out loud she said, "It's illegal to talk that way nowadays, Dr. A."

"Oh, I didn't mean anything by it."

"Well, we don't talk dirt in this department. Just in case you didn't know."

Phillip pulled back and left, giving Trish a wink.

We only hired him because we were desperate after Charlie had a stroke, and the budget was so damn tight. I did say, when we were discussing him, that I didn't have a good gut feeling on whether he was legit. And the guys poo-pooed me.

Just then Clare Conner, MD, her best gal friend in the department, walked in. "Trish, you're always going on about how you feel about that guy. Just look at the data. He has quite a few publications."

"Did you notice the titles? Four or five are about sexual performance."

"Are you for or against it, Trish?"

Trish blushed. "None of your business," she quipped and continued. "I can't believe he slicks his hair back like Rudolph Valentino from ancient movie times, Clare. And there's something oily about him. Even Sheila told me shortly after he arrived that she would never allow herself to be alone with the jerk."

"What caused that reaction?" Clare asked.

"She was putting his mail in his box. There were a lot of periodicals and she dropped them. A couple of the brown paper coverings ripped, revealing porno magazines. That really blew Sheila's mind."

"Well, let's stay out of it, Trish, and let the chief handle him. We needed help desperately in the Psychopharm Unit, and he's taken over several lecture topics for the residents."

"Has he said anything to you out of the way, Clare?"

"Nope, but I feel like he's undressing me with his eyes sometimes."

"Well, you are nice-looking."

"Trish, I've been around the block a few times, and this guy is a little creepy."

"Okay, point taken. I avoid Phillip Atwater as much as possible, too. His name should really be 'Asswater,' or better yet 'Assbutt.' I'll call him a polite 'Dr. A,' But, not by his first name."

❋

At least Steven and I can have a nice evening. Trish thought.

It was late afternoon and Trish, having changed clothes, was feeling spiffy when Steven pulled into her drive and rang the door bell. She quickly opened the door.

"Hungry?"

"You bet!"

"Let's roll!"

Guido's was well-known on the Coast. An old house with a wraparound porch, now enclosed and air-conditioned, it was a favorite of Trish's since childhood, where special occasion meals were held.

"Drink?"

"No, I'll have wine with dinner."

"I think I can manage that." Steven smiled at her, taking her hand across the table.

He really is a very nice man, and sincere. I have a good feeling about him in my gut.

She turned over his hand, "You have some calluses here. Still working out?"

"Yep, three times a week at Premier."

"It's pretty busy there. Do many women use Premier?"

"A few."

"Are they knockouts?"

"I never noticed."

"Oh, yeah? I hear that's where the fanny flossers hang, looking for fresh meat."

"Fanny flossers? Fresh meat? Whatever are you talking about, Trish?"

"Thong workout clothes! It's a meat market. Subconsciously or not, they're probably looking for new conquests."

"Can it, Trish! That's beneath you. It's just the least expensive place to train."

"Ever see Priscilla Smith there?"

"Priscilla who?"

"The gal I introduced you to that time we were together in Winn Dixie."

"Oh, her! Come to think of it, maybe a few times, but I usually go early, like 6 a.m. What's your interest in her?"

"Oh, she called and wanted to talk to me about something personal. She didn't want to see me as a patient, which I wouldn't do anyway because of our prior relationship."

"How do you handle that, what I mean—when a friend or acquaintance is depressed and wants to see you as a patient?"

"I tell them the truth. I'd rather be their friend than their therapist, and I give three names of competent therapists, sometimes not even other psychiatrists. There are lots of fine psychotherapists around. Probably more of the good therapists are actually non-MD types. Anyway, Priscilla's coming over Sunday afternoon to have lemonade."

"Guess that means you won't be sailing with us guys."

"I think three strong men can handle the boat."

FOURTEEN

Saturday, Trish awoke to the sound of the yard crew mowing the grass.

"Oh, my! It's 9 a.m."

Smiling, she rolled out of bed, dislodging Smoke from his sleeping place behind the crook of her knees.

"That was a pleasant time last night. Think I'm getting more interested."

The phone rang. "Dr. Trish?"

"Yes?"

"Sorry to bother you on a Saturday, you not being my backup and all—" It was Dora, a second year resident. "I've been trying for two hours to get Dr. Atwater, and he just doesn't answer his phone or his beeper. And the ER docs are on my case to move a couple of patients out of there."

That twerp! He's done this before!

"Shoot."

"The patient is a 35-year-old, white female, named Bridget Johnson who was brought in by the sheriff because her family called and said she was going to kill herself."

"How?"

"By taking all her pills."

"Did she take any?" Trish popped open a can of V-8.

"No. They got the bottle away from her before she could."

"What was the urine drug screen?"

"Positive for THC, and she had a blood alcohol of 175."

"How's she now?"

"Great. Says it was a dumb thing to do. Says she goes to

the mental health clinic and sees a social worker. Promises she'll go in Monday for an extra session if I let her go."

"I'm familiar with Bridget. Did an eval on her myself a year or so ago. She's done this before, but never takes the pills. So, in this case, you can send her out. Be sure to document that you discussed the case with me. Get the chart to me and I'll co-sign it and write a note that I talked to you about it. Who's coming in today to round with you?"

"Dr. Hawthorn, but he's not here yet, and they really wanted me to get her out of here. He'll be here by 10:30, I'm sure, and maybe we can move a couple more or possibly discharge one I admitted last night, if he has sobered up."

"Okay, bye now."

"Sorry to bother you."

"No problem. Don't let the turkeys get you down."

That damned ass, Atwater.

Retrieving the paper from outside the front door, she settled on the sofa with the V-8 and green tea.

'New Orleans Vice Squad Investigation Underway' caught Trish's eye.

"Well, well. The beat goes on."

'Police reluctant to give this reporter details of a current investigation, saying only it may be far-reaching and could involve public figures who would not welcome the publicity or any upcoming criminal charges.'

❋

FIFTEEN

Skip, barking furiously, announced Priscilla's arrival.

"I hear, I hear. Yes, I understand the chimes hurt your ears. Hush, hush."

Skip quieted, wagging his tail as Priscilla stepped inside the front door.

"What a charming home you have. So comfortable. I like it. And who is this? What's your name?"

"His name is Skip, rescued puppy from the pound. Down, down, Skip!" Skip danced about and sat for Priscilla to pet him.

"Such a nice dog. Reggie doesn't like dogs. Won't let us have one."

"Well, at least Skip gives you his approval. I trust his instincts about people, almost more than my own."

More evidence that husband Reggie really runs the show.

"Come on back. I've made some lemonade with real lemons. But, I used artificial sweetener."

"Great! It's like a stroll down memory lane to have lemonade. My grandmother used to make it on Sunday afternoons, and we'd sit under the ceiling fan on the screened porch and nibble on her tea cakes."

"I have some of those also."

"You baked them?"

"No. I liberated them from the freezer. Mama made them last spring. Hope they're still okay?"

"Oh, I'm sure they are."

Not one to mince around, Trish said, "What's up, Prissy?

I haven't seen you much over the years. Our paths seem to have taken different directions."

"Yes, that's true. Oh, Trish! Please keep this to yourself, but I'm so upset about something Reggie is suggesting. It's just too horrifying! Oh, I'm crying now. Do you have any tissues? Thanks. I should first tell you I really do try to be a good Christian wife to Reggie. He drinks a lot, more and more as the years go by. I was only able to come over this afternoon because he's asleep."

"Passed out, you mean."

"Well, I guess so. Anyway, he controls me so much. Now, I really believe what the bible says, that the husband is the head of the household and the authority in the home. But he's so jealous and suspicious. I get to go to the Garden Club because it's only women, and if he knew I was going to the gym where men work out, he would have a fit.

"Anyway, now it's getting so bad. I don't dare cross him. It's like walking on eggshells, or better yet, splintered glass. I'm very careful, I don't want to get hurt, but one little step he sees as out of line, and he blows up. So far, he hasn't broken anything but I'm afraid there are more than bruises in my future if things don't change. My church doesn't believe in divorce and, in a way, I still love him, but that's not what I came to talk to you about."

"Okay I'm here for you. Take your time."

"The other night…in fact, it was the night before I called you…he came home late, 10 p.m. Said he had business. I'm beginning to be suspicious about "business." He said he'd met a fellow from your department at lunch. Shared a table 'cause there was a crowd and they got to talking."

"What was his name, did he say?"

"Atwater, I think."

Jesus, what's he up to?

"He told Reggie he was doing some kind of sexual performance research and was looking for volunteers, that he'd pay $100 an hour to video couples doing, ummm, you know, kinky things, and Reggie wants us to do it. Trish, I can't do that! No matter how much money! Oh dear, I'm using all your tissues."

"That's okay, go on."

"He said they didn't do it at the medical center. He has a studio over by Pass Christian. Trish, does the medical center sanction research like that? I knew you'd know."

"Not that I know about."

"Do you know a Dr. Atwater?"

"Yes, there's a faculty member by that name in the department. Not one of my favorite people. But we're a small department, and everyone knows pretty much what kind of research everyone else does. I know he had a couple of research papers on his C.V. that had to do with sexual matters, something about desensitizing pedophiles with visual images. But, I've not heard of anything new since he came here a couple of years ago."

"Oh, Trish. What am I going to do? I can't even conceive of doing anything like that, and Reggie will kill me if I refuse."

"Do you mean that?"

"Well, maybe not kill me but assault me, give me a black eye, and, oh, the embarrassment!"

"Don't do anything. Just avoid that topic, and if push comes to shove, have a headache or stomach flu or something. You need a contingency plan. Do you have someplace to go if you feel you're in danger?"

"My sister lives up at Hattiesburg. I could stay with her for a while."

"Have you ever worked?"

"No, Reggie wouldn't let me."

"Do you have any job skills?"

"Not really. I never learned to type. Gardening isn't much of a job skill. I know how to cook a little."

"Looks like you need to think about getting some job training. Do you know how to use a computer?"

"No, Reggie…"

"I know. Reggie says, 'Don't bother your pretty little head about things like that.'"

"How did you know?"

"Just a guess. They have computers at the public library. You can go there while he's at work and they'll show you how to use one. They probably have a program where you can teach yourself to type."

"Oh, Trish! That would be wonderful. Do you think I could do that?"

"Sure. You're not stupid, Prissy. You've just never given yourself a chance."

"Oh, I feel so much better. Do you think we could be friends? I mean, I'm a nobody, and you're a big fancy professor but…"

"I'd like that. I need to connect with people outside the medical field. We'll start doing some things together. Meanwhile, I'll look into what Dr. Ass has been up to."

"Dr. Ass?"

"That's what I call Atwater behind his back."

"Oh, that's rare!"

"I've always thought he was a little weird."

"Sorry, I was so upset and sniffling. You won't get in trouble for checking on him, will you?"

"No problem there. I rank higher than he does. I have tenure."

"Tenure? What's that?"

"Well, it actually means they can't fire me. I guess if I screwed a patient on the front lawn of the clinic, they would find a way, but short of that, my position on the faculty is secure. Mostly, I can rest on my laurels and only do things I'm interested in doing."

"That's terrific, Trish. Wish I had done more. Gee, it's almost five, I'd better get home. Reggie will be waking up, if he hasn't already, and I need to get started on supper. These days, he doesn't eat like he used to. Beer seems to be his main food, but Junior really puts away the vittles. It's amazing how much that boy can eat! Growing like a weed! Thanks again. Bye for now."

Skip wagged his tail, and Smoke twined around Priscilla's legs one last time as she departed.

"Well, looks like you two have given your marks of approval to Prissy.

"Gosh, her life must be awful, and I thought I had it tough with ol' Larry. And to think she thought Reggie was her soul mate in high school.

"Wonder why they never had any other children after Junior? Don't look at me like that, Skip. We don't need any puppies or kittens to be accountable for. I'm a responsible pet owner. That's why you two are neutered."

❁

SIXTEEN

When Trish arrived the next morning at 8:10, the department was quiet. Office staff was not due until 8:30, and those assigned to inpatient coverage on the psych unit were already at the hospital. Trish put a sticky note on Clare's door, asking her to stop by her office first thing.

It was 11:30 when Clare knocked. "Sorry to be late, Trish. I'm just not a morning person. Glad I can do consultation rounds in the afternoon."

"It's nice to have flexibility and not punch in like the support staff. Come on in, I need to talk to you about something. Close the door. Here, let me turn on the sound box."

"Trish, are you getting paranoid in your old age? Put it on 'gentle stream,' if you feel the need. Those gulls and ocean waves are too much for Monday morning."

"Sure, your call. Look, Clare, these walls really aren't soundproof. That's part of why they don't want us to see patients here in our offices, and I am beginning to believe there are some very snoopy people around here."

"In that case, turn up the volume and shoot."

"What do you know about Phil Atwater?"

"Dr. Ass? Nothing, other than he's a slick, slimy creep as we have discussed before. And remember, I told you he's always showing up when I least expect him, and that I feel he's undressing me when he looks at me."

"Clare, you're a very attractive blonde with good skin, long legs, and the body of a 21-year-old swimmer. I hate you for that. Well, not really."

"Trish, the hair color is from a bottle, remember? I'm a Dallas native, land of big blonde hair. More bleach is sold in Big D than anywhere else in the country."

"Steve was very appreciative of your looks last spring when you went sailing with us."

"Is something developing there? Oh, I hope so. I think he could be Mr. Right for you."

"Maybe. Yes, maybe. Now back to Dr. Ass. Is he doing any sexual research that you know of?"

"No. He takes one or two patients who need a year of therapy before they can get the sex change surgery in New Orleans. Seems that he has published a couple of papers along those lines, but our dean, with his background, would never approve anything more than that. Why do you ask?"

"An acquaintance from high school came by yesterday, all upset. Seems her boozer of a husband met Phil over lunch when they had to share a table, and he asked him if he and his wife would do some sexual acts for video recording. Said it was research. But the funny thing is, he said the studio was over by Pass Christian.

"The boozer wants to do it. Says it's good money, $100 an hour, and Prissy is terrified, not only of the idea, but also of her husband. He's abusive to her. She's stayed in the marriage all these years because of her religious beliefs, and there's a boy. Junior is 16 or 17."

"Why am I not surprised? This is just the kind of thing Dr. Ass would do, if you ask me."

"And last Saturday, I had a call from the on-call resident. Dr. Ass was her backup. It was 8 a.m., and he wasn't answering his beeper or the phone."

"Trish that happened to me, too. I wonder if he's sloughed off on anyone else. Should we tell the Chair?"

"Don't waste your breath. Wouldn't surprise me if Dennis is involved. He puts on a good front, sweet wife and little kids…"

"Trish!"

"He hired Dr. Ass. Okay, I'll let that go. Where does Dr. Ass live anyway?"

"Beats me. I think he has a condo and no girlfriend or wife, I've ever heard mentioned. He certainly doesn't strike me as a closet queen."

"You'd think he'd buy a house. Most do after a year or so, and he's been here two years now, at least. But maybe that would interfere with his lifestyle? He sure drives an expensive car, a new Porsche. Keep your eyes open, Clare, and let me know if you hear anything. I'm beginning to smell a rat in a woodpile."

"Sure thing, Trish. And if you think I can be helpful to your friend—Prissy, is it—to see her as a patient or as another supportive gal friend, let me know."

"Okay. By the way, how's your better half?"

"Sam? Oh, he's fine. Not on drugs, no legal problems, not boozing, loves me and the practice of cardiology. Kids are fine, too."

"Great. You better run. Catch you later."

❈

Hot, humid steam prevailed as Trish pulled into the parking lot at the clinic. Her spot with shade taken, she cracked the windows of the new T-Bird, and popped open her golf umbrella for protection from the sun, breathing a sigh of relief upon entering the cool interior of the building. A few minutes later, Clyde poked his head through her open doorway. Trish usually left her door open. Closing it the day of the murder had varied from her routine.

"What's up?" piped Clyde. "Not much."

"Sleeping okay?"

"Yeah. Doesn't seem I'm going to have post-traumatic stress disorder from seeing Hilda's body."

"Did you know her?"

"No, but my mother had spoken to her a few times at the

Garden Club. Any news from your side? How's the investigation going? Any suspects?"

"None. Her ex was out of the country. But, she did have a whack to the back of the head before being placed in the bathtub. The word is the coroner thinks she was probably unconscious and that she would have died from the head wound anyway, without treatment."

"Then her throat was slit?"

"Yep, and as we both know, it required strength and rage. And by the way, right-handedness marks the killer."

"Oh, that's new information. Did they find a weapon?"

"Nope, but whatever it was, it was very sharp. Probably the killer wrapped it in something. No prints on the door that haven't been identified. Using a couple of paper towels would prevent that, and there were plenty of those available."

"Had the security system been reset?"

"Yep. Nothing out of the ordinary on the monitor at Bayou Security that night."

"Think they'll solve this case?"

"Sure. It just might take some time."

"Clyde, ever heard of a Notti's?"

"Nope. Why?"

"Just curious. Someone found a business card with a number on it, a Biloxi number, and wondered what it was. Maybe some sort of private business?"

"Did you call the number?"

"Yes, but it was an answering machine."

"Did you check that cross-street directory for a street address?"

"Yes, and nothing there. Is there any way you could check and find out for me where the telephone statement goes?"

"Sure. It might take a few days. Don't want that piss detective to think I'm doing anything out of the ordinary."

"Thanks, Clyde. How's vice on the Coast these days?"

"Vice? Are you looking for some action, Dr. Trish?"

"Now, Clyde, you know me better than that. No. What's

the word on the street? Is there much prostitution, porno stuff, skin-flicks—stuff like that?"

"Things seem to be quiet lately."

"That doesn't mean nothing's going on."

"Dr. Trish, it surely is but most likely it's undercover. We don't take no truck with behavior like that out in the open-like. There's enough to satisfy anybody over New Orleans way."

"The casinos, do you think they make a difference?"

"Probably not. It was good for their business when they figured a way to float those gambling boats on an itty bit of water and stay in port. Kept them poor gamblers from getting seasick. Don't think they have caused an increase in the amount of vice.

"From my side of things it seems like we have more drugs, crack especially, but that could have happened anyway; just a sign of the times."

"The casinos sure made a lot more money when they didn't have to go out past the three mile limit, and money seems to be a driving force in these parts. Ever been on the gambling boats in the old days when they went out, Dr. Trish?"

"No. I have enough sin in my life already."

"Sin? What are you talking about? You seem to be a mighty fine lady."

"Thanks, Clyde, but you'll never know, and I won't tell you."

"It's none of my business anyway. Took the wife out to a casino once for her birthday. Gave her fifty dollars to play with and she lost it all. Think that cured her. She was mad as a wet hen for a week, and I surely didn't see how it was fun to give your money away. Some of those folks sitting at those machines looked like they were in a trance, and they sure didn't look like they were having any fun to me. Like they say, 'To each his own,' and that ain't nothing I'm interested in doing."

"I'm with you, Clyde!"

After Clyde left, Trish wondered if Hilda liked to go to the casinos.

That's something I need to check out. Maybe Prissy would know. I'll ask her next time I see her.

❋

Trish had survived the dog days of August and continued to be curious about Hilda's murder.

"Smithe residence, lady of the house speaking," Prissy murmured into the receiver in a soft drawl. It was the Saturday before Labor Day.

"Got anything going Labor Day, Prissy? Trish here."

"Oh, hi, Trish! So glad you called. No, nothing special. Junior is going over to Gulf Hills with a group of boys on the football team, and Reggie will probably just drink beer here."

"I was thinking of barbequing a couple of chickens. Want to come over?"

"I don't know. Reggie will be tying one on that day."

"I have a date with Steven for sailing in the afternoon. You could drop by my house around 7 p.m. and meet him."

"That might work. Reggie will be soused out in the recliner by then."

❋

The Labor Day sail out to Ship Island was pleasant, especially because the guys ran the boat, and Trish didn't have to do anything.

Bob, one of the crew, noted, "Something is brewing out in the Gulf."

"No way! I saw the weather channel this morning," replied Trish.

"Don't care. Something is building up. I can feel it."

"No need to take her out of the water yet," said Steven, as they secured the boat, locking the hatch and storing the big genoa and spinnaker sails inside the cabin. "I'll keep an eye on the weather reports and call you guys if we have to tow/trailer her up to my brother's place in Forest County."

Steven took no chances after the damage from the last hurricane, and his brother's large barn easily held the boat and trailer, although it was a chore to lower the mast for the trip.

On the way home Trish said, "Prissy is coming over for a little visit about seven to eat barbeque chicken with us."

"Great. Want me to do the grilling? That's something I'm pretty good at."

"Sure."

"Okay, I'll drop you off and be back in a few, shipshape and ready to do duty over the coals."

❖

SEVENTEEN

"Come on in, Prissy," Trish said, standing in the doorway, holding Smoke.

"Steven's out back with the chickens. Never saw a man get so involved with a couple of chickens. He says he has a secret sauce. I guess it's a man thing."

"Thanks, I've been so upset about the way Reggie has been acting. Glad to come over to visit with you. If he isn't drinking and passing out—he calls it sleeping—he's gone and not home 'til late. Friday night he never came home and wouldn't give an answer. 'None of your damn business' was all he said, and he followed that with, 'Do I need to straighten you out?'

"Trish, I was so scared, I just got out of his way as quick as I could. Reminded me of the way my daddy was when I was a girl. That's why I never had any friends over in high school. You could never tell what kind of mood he would be in. Many was the time I saw bruises on my mama. The little ones were scared most of the time. I even asked mama why she didn't leave him.

"She said, 'We don't do that in our family.' "Even if he beats you?" I would ask.

"And she always said 'I'll get my reward in heaven. Blessed are the meek.'"

"Is that the way you feel, Prissy?"

"I always have, but now, with Reggie acting the way he has, I'm beginning to think otherwise. Trish, do you think he's having an affair?"

"It's certainly possible. Have you ever suspected anything in the past?"

"Maybe a few times over the years. He was always so demanding, in a sexual way, if you know what I mean, and then there were those times he seemed distant. Actually, that was a relief."

"Have you been checked by your doctor?"

"What do you mean?"

"Well, he could have brought you a little present you didn't know about or want."

"Oh my God! I'm down for my annual next week. I'll ask her to check for anything then."

"Good. At least that's something you can do. Did you find out anything about Hilda?"

"I asked Reggie, and he overheard some guys at his gym talking about her murder, but really, Trish, he was guarded and didn't say much. I think he saw her there, 'cause he goes there before he starts drinking for the day, so that means late morning or early afternoon."

"That would fit, since she was a gardener. Outside work would have to be done in the early morning before the heat built up, or late in the afternoon when the sun was low. So, she might have worked out midday, to get the benefit of the air-conditioned gym."

"Trish, a week or so ago, while digging in my flower bed, I found a key. It looks like a key to a door lock. Like on a house, maybe. I did that bed very carefully last spring and I'm almost certain that if it had been there then, I would have found it."

"Did you try it on your door?"

"Yes, but it didn't fit. But the name on the key was 'Schlager,' the same as our door lock, so it must be to a house."

"Not necessarily. Maybe you should try it on some other locks."

"Which ones?"

"How about Reggie's office?"

"Okay. Any other suggestions?"

"I have a wild idea. Do you know where Hilda lived?"

"No, but I can look it up in the Garden Club yearbook."

"Try the key there."

"Do you think anyone is watching her place?"

"Probably not. Her family probably cleared her things out and it's rented or sold to someone else by now. I'll come with you."

"The locks might have been changed."

"We won't know unless we try. Are you game?"

"Sure. Call me when you can go. Can you get away during the week?"

"I'll call around 11:30, and we can loop by and see if there are any new tenants. If so, they probably wouldn't be home in the middle of the day anyway."

"I'd better get home before Reggie wakes up. I'll tell him I've been to the library. That's where I usually go on Monday night. Wonder if it was open, today being Labor Day? I'll call later in the week."

"Take care."

"Sure thing."

EIGHTEEN

Smoke meowed, and Skip wagged his tail.

"All right! Okay! I forgot to put out food when I came in. Better late than never. You're both fat enough anyway," said Trish as she filled the bowls with dry food.

She flipped on the TV. The weather channel boomed, and yes, there was an update—*tropical low developing off the Yucatan Peninsula of Mexico.*

That Bob! He's really something. How'd he know something was up? Another mystery of life.

Gathering the trash, she took the large black bag out through the garage to the curb. Dusk gathered, and she noticed the evening star Venus. Repeating the childhood verse, "Star light, star bright, first star I see tonight. I wish I may, I wish I might…." Her mind drew a blank as the garage door rumbled closed for the remainder of the poem.

❋

It was Tuesday morning at the Smith house when Junior said "Our first game is this Friday. Think ya'll can come?"

"I'll be there. I can't say about your daddy. He might have to work."

Prissy heard the note of hope in Junior's voice. Reggie managed to almost always claim a conflict with whatever Junior's activity happened to be.

Poor kid. He adores his dad and certainly didn't deserve this.

The few times Reggie had showed up, Junior's joy was

evident. Later he chattered, in high spirits, only to cry with disappointment at the next missed event.

"He has to make money to take care of us and this nice house."

"Mama, I don't even have a car."

"Let's not get started on that one. Off with you." Prissy rushed Junior out the door.

Pouring a second cup of coffee, Priscilla sat at the kitchen table reading her bible. For a moment she felt numb and tears filled her eyes, the words blurring on the page.

They were just words.

I've followed all the rules! And I still have this empty feeling. Somehow that's not going to be enough.

The thought became more formed, a bubble of awareness about to pop up in a pot of water on the boil.

Is that what I am, a pot of water ready to boil?

She sniffed and retrieving a tissue from the pocket of her robe blew her nose. She felt somewhat better.

If this pot is going to boil over, it better have room to overflow. What does that mean for me? First off, I'd have to make some money. What am I really good at? All that comes to mind is that I make excellent chicken salad sandwiches, and Junior says my chocolate chip cookies are the best. The gals at the Garden Club rave about the chicken salad sandwiches, especially when they're on homemade bread. But how to make money with that?

Hearing Reggie in the shower, she hurriedly dressed and left a note by the coffee pot—'Gone to the grocery store. See you tonight.'

At least this way I don't have to talk to him.

On the way to the Winn-Dixie, she passed several construction sites—new houses. It hit her. Those men ate lunch, and they probably had money.

Maybe they would buy my chicken salad sandwiches and chocolate chip cookies. Nothing ventured, nothing gained.

She added to the grocery list the ingredients for the two

items. Her mood considerably lighter, she spent the remainder of the day making bread, chicken salad, and cookies.

I really shouldn't do this alone. Let's see how much money I've spent.

With her hand-held calculator she tallied the cost of the ingredients guessing at what she had on hand.

Maybe old Mrs. Gray would ride with her. Mrs. Gray, in her 70s but still spry, frequently asked Priscilla over for coffee, but Priscilla had generally avoided her because of nosey questions. Sure enough, Mrs. Gray was delighted to 'ride shotgun,' as she put it, and even suggested prices for the venture.

"Are you sure that's not too much?"

"Have you checked the prices of a plain ole sandwich at the Muffin Man lately?"

"No."

"Well, this ain't too much, especially for homemade."

The next day, to Priscilla's amazement, the sandwiches and cookies sold after two hours, and she pocketed forty dollars.

When I get a hundred, I'll open a bank account. Oh, Reggie would just have a fit. What he doesn't know won't hurt him.

I sure better not let him know what I'm doing. He'd be sure to accuse me of picking up men for sex or some such. Maybe I won't be so dependent on Reggie now—forty dollars isn't much, but it's a start.

I have enough to make another run. Might as well see how much I can sell.

She began to happily hum *Rock Of Ages* under her breath.

❀

NINETEEN

"Trish, it's me. About our key plans—I'm doing something new, so could I pick you up outside the medical school about eleven on Thursday?"

"Something new? What are you up to?"

"I was thinking about how I could make some money of my own. I decided to make cookies and sandwiches and sell them to men working on building sites. Reggie keeps track of every penny I spend. This way, I can put a little away on the side. I've already cleared over a hundred dollars this week!"

"What brought all this about?"

"I'll tell you Thursday. Will you ride with me first, and then we can go by where Hilda lived?"

"Sure thing."

And I was thinking Prissy a passive little Southern belle. There's a lot more to Ms. Priscilla than I gave her credit.

Trish waited in the shade until Priscilla pulled up.

"God! What's all that in the back seat? Have you been to Wal-Mart? Must have cleaned the place out!" The back seat was full of lumpy plastic bags.

"Those are the sandwiches and cookies. I save plastic bags and they work just fine."

"There must be fifty bags back there!"

"That's right. Word must be getting around. We'll be finished in a couple of hours and I'll have you back by two for sure," said Prissy.

The run of the building sites route went quickly, and with

the money carefully placed in a Ziploc plastic bag under her car seat, Priscilla headed to the street where Hilda had lived.

"Do you have the key?" asked Trish. "It's in my pocket."

"Still no idea how it got in the flower bed?"

"No. The flower bed is by the front walk."

Twenty minutes later, in front of the townhouse, Trish said, "Why are we doing this?"

"I'm not sure. It was your idea"

They walked up to the front door. "I guess everybody around here is at work. Try the key."

"Nope, it doesn't fit. Maybe someone else lives here and changed the locks."

"Maybe, but it looks empty," said Trish, peeking in the small window of the front door.

"Can I help you?"

The deep voice caused Trish and Priscilla to jump. Turning, they saw a large, rawboned woman, who could have passed for a man, standing on the front lawn next door.

"We were just seeing if anyone was home," said Trish.

"Not likely. She died earlier this summer. Did you know Hilda?"

"No, someone told us a person at this address might buy sandwiches and cookies from us," Prissy quickly inserted. "We thought we'd check. Bye now."

Trish took Priscilla by the arm, ushering her to the car, "That was a pretty weak explanation. Where'd she come from?"

"He or she? Did you see the arms on her! Looked like a weightlifter."

"She must have been looking out her window when we drove up."

"Well, at least we know the key isn't to Hilda's condo. Now what?"

"Hell, I don't know! Just keep the key."

"Trish, you really shouldn't say hell."

"Look, Prissy. I'm beginning to like you, and I'm thinking

we can be good friends. You'll just have to put up with occasional colorful language on my part."

"Sure, sure. Call me if you think of anything. If Reggie answers, hang up."

TWENTY

Back in Trish's office, Clare burst in. "Have you heard the news? Dennis is no longer our chairman!"

"Saints preserve us. No longer the boss?"

"Yep. The dean called him in this morning about 10:00 and relieved him of the chairmanship."

"Oh, wow! He's tenured so he'll be around for a while until he finds something else. He would never stay as just a professor."

"What do you think happened, Clare?"

"I think it's about some funny business with the money that comes in to the Psychopharm Research Unit from the drug companies. Bet there's been some improper shifting from account to account," said Clare her hand on her hip and her head cocked. "How else is all his travel paid for?"

"It might have to do with billing. Remember how he was saying a year or so ago that our services deserved to be billed at a higher rate because we were experts?"

"Did you buy that, Clare?"

"No, I didn't. I sure hope you didn't either."

"Give me credit, but I wouldn't put it past some of the guys doing it. Talk about risk management. Could be big trouble for the entire medical school."

"Maybe there's been a further internal audit Trish and the dean wants to mend fences before the feds come nosing around."

"Maybe he and Dr. Ass have been up to something really illegal."

"What are you getting at?"

"I keep coming back to how Dennis recruited him. And how Dr. Ass asked the husband of a friend of mine if he were interested in performing sexual acts with my friend for a video disguised as research."

"There isn't any research going on in that area or we would know about it. This department isn't that big."

"Ever wonder what Dr. Ass does in his spare time? He sure doesn't cover his backup call assignments."

"Trish! Something just came to me."

"What?"

"You know I drive a Porsche, too, like Dr. A. Mine is ancient, but still good, and we go to the same place to have them serviced—oil change, etc. This summer, back in July, I was having the oil changed and chatting with the oil change man. He knows where I work and that I'm a psychiatrist.

"He said, 'There's two of you psychiatrists who drive a Porsche.' I played dumb, 'Yes, the other one is a man.'

"'He's in here a lot more often than you are,' he said, and puts the miles on his. I bet he's in here three times to your one.'

"What do you make of that?"

"I'd say nothing until all this hit the fan. He told Reggie the research place was over by Pass Christian, and it's only a little farther to the 'Big Easy.'"

"And remember, Dr. Ass sees an occasional sex change patient for psychotherapy for the required year or so."

"I'd bet money that Dr. Ass has boundary problems. Probably takes patients to dinner or worse. Sure hope it doesn't get back to the residents," said Trish.

"He's so oily."

"I'd say slimy. Always those little innuendos and the way he puts a sexual connotation on the most innocent statements."

"It's like his mind is between his legs."

"Do you think he's gay?"

"Not gay like my male friends, who are straight about their orientation and are productive citizens, who just happen to be gay. Maybe he's AC/DC."

"I wouldn't put it past him to engage in any sexual perversion that comes down the pike, from bestiality to anything alive or dead, animate or inanimate."

"God! Trish, you're really laying a trip on him."

"It would be easy to say he was just a bad seed. But we both know there was probably childhood neglect and abuse, for him to turn out this way."

"He's so well defended, it would take years of therapy for him to become aware of how low his self-esteem really is."

"I'm not sure he'd ever engage in a therapeutic alliance with a therapist to start with. Might pretend he has and then ask them out—male or female. Probably both."

"Major boundary problems. His internal trash is probably why in the beginning he went into psychiatry. We always have a few of that type around here. Well, now that we've run an analysis of Dr. Ass, I suppose it's time we ceased this chit chat and earned our keep."

Stopping by Sheila's office, Trish said, "I'm on my way to the mental health clinic. It's my day."

"Oh, Dr. Trish, is it still creepy over there?"

"Not any more creepy than anywhere else around here. So much has happened around this place over the years; rapes, murder. I don't let it bother me that much."

"Sometimes it bothers me. I've avoided that hall near hospital administration where the university police shot and killed that prisoner patient who tried to escape after picking up a gun left for him in the toilet. One of the secretaries from that area told me blood was everywhere. I took a long route for six months."

"At least that terracotta tile cleans up well and they even repainted that area a different color and added a wallpaper border. So no reminders left."

"Dr. Trish," Sheila said in her shaming tone, as she placed the messages taken off the answering machine on the desk.

"If you must know, Sheila, I'm using the downstairs toilet for the time being, but I wouldn't want just anyone to know, not that you would think bad of me."

"God love you, still remember the sight, do you?"

"Not to the extreme, Sheila, did you ever notice by saying 'God love him or her' first, most anything is excused? Even terrible cruel things are accepted. Now, I understand you weren't meaning to criticize me, but think about it. Sorry to preach, but things we would never say straight out, are excused if we preface it with 'God love you.'"

"That's true, Dr. Trish. I wonder where that came from?"

"Beats me, Sheila. I've delayed enough. I'm off to the clinic. There's only one of these messages I need to answer."

❁

TWENTY-ONE

"Hi, Clyde! Keeping watch on the front door?"

"Sure thing, Dr. Trish. Actually, it's pretty quiet around here these days."

"Any news on the murder?"

"Did you hear there were some THC metabolites in her urine? She liked to live better chemically."

"No, anything else?"

"Benzos in the blood and a low alcohol level."

"Wow! Never would have taken her for a druggie. Do they know when she was put into the tub?"

"Coroner says about six to eight, maybe ten, hours before she was discovered."

"Any new unusual fingerprints? I saw the technicians all over the place."

"Nope, 'pears the killer wore gloves. The guess is he took them off at the site so as not to drip any blood, and he may have worn another pair out of the building. There were mighty few drops of blood, in spite of the arterial spatter on the tub enclosure."

"Anybody see a car early that morning? Did ya'll question neighbors or folks working nearby?"

"Sure thing, Dr. Trish, but no leads there."

"Doesn't the department record someone entering the building early or late?"

"Nope, this security system is old. It only goes off at Bayou Security if the alarm isn't turned off within fifteen seconds with a security key."

"Are there many of those around? Seems I remember only a few of the staff have a master key. It wouldn't be hard to make a copy."

"There are more of those keys around than you think. On weekends, groundskeepers and the like come inside for supplies kept in the closet on the first floor, where they store the floor polishing equipment, extra paper towels, and stuff like that. Oh, I forgot to tell you. The post said the weapon was a large knife, probably a sharp kitchen knife, and that quite a bit of force was used to do that much damage with one slash."

"Well, enough on that subject. Let me see if my first patient is a no-show. Wife still baking cakes?"

"Yes ma'am. Need one? Her Better Than Sex cake almost is. She has quite a little business built up since word got out how good hers are."

"Looks as if you've enjoyed a few yourself."

"Oh, this is just a little middle-aged spread starting at 40. This hair of mine started turning white when I was 35. Must be the stress of police work."

"Maybe so."

The key from Prissy's flower bed came into Trish's mind.

Well, that was a flop, Dr. Sleuth. Better stick to medical sleuthing.

Academic psychiatry isn't the low stress job some people think. Especially when dealing with a suicidal, self-mutilating borderline. They give me a stiff neck.

❁

TWENTY-TWO

"Good week?" asked Prissy.

"Yeah, but I'm taking a few hours of annual leave this afternoon; mental health time for myself. Follow my T-Bird to my house, so we can talk."

Fifteen minutes later, under the overhead fan, with Diet Cokes in hand and Smoke in Trish's lap, talk began.

"Business still good?"

"Oh yes! Going great guns. I'm a little tired, staying up late and getting up early to make the sandwiches. I'm almost to the point of needing help."

"What about your housekeeper?"

"Maybe, but she only comes every now and then."

"It's funny to me Prissy that Reggie will pay for her occasionally and yet not want you to do things you want to."

"That's true. He wants me to just be the lady of the house. I'm thinking about leaving him. There's more to life than this. If he knew what I was up to, making money, he would say, 'That's beneath your station in life.'"

Prissy gently stroked Smoke who moved to her lap.

"That's so old-fashioned. Ever hear of woman's lib? You have a business and are about to expand. I think you have a niche in the market.

"The wife of one of the policemen who works security at the clinic bakes cakes to sell. Maybe she'd be interested. Want her number?"

"Yeah, it's better this way. I'd hate her to call and Reggie answer the phone. By the way, I saw the funniest thing today,

Trish. I was out delivering the sandwiches, and I noticed a group of people working on the flower beds at the welfare office. The place people go to register for their food stamps."

"So, what's funny about that?"

"I noticed them, because they all had on the same color tee-shirts, bright Kelly green. Remember that woman who scared the bejesus out of us at Hilda's condo? I could have sworn she was one of those workers, and she was equal to the men. Really looked like a football player, but I'm sure she was a gal 'cause her tee-shirt was tight, and you could see the bra straps and back band."

"And you saw all that riding by the food stamp office?"

"There was a red light and I was stopped anyway. And, the weird thing was, she looked up and our eyes met briefly. Gave me the creeps! I don't think she recognized me."

"It was probably that civic club, the Green Garden Gang, that does beautification projects. You'd never catch me out in that heat. I hate to sweat."

"But, Trish, your yard looks so nice."

"Most of that is thanks to the neighborhood yard team. I inherited them when I moved into this place."

"What do you mean?"

"Shortly after I was settled, I was out front one day and this neat truck stopped, driven by a polite, middle-aged, black man, who said he had a team that did most of the houses on the block. Been mowing for years and that the previous owners used him. So, I signed up, and he keeps the front looking really good, mows and does the edging, and he'll rake the leaves and put down pine straw in the fall. Does flower beds, too, but that's extra."

"Looks like the storm is going to miss us this time."

"Last I heard, it had moved onto the Mexican shore."

"I'm not complaining."

"We could use some rain. Bet this one's too far away for that."

"By the way, what's your yardman's name?"

"Curtis. I bet there aren't too many white women around doing yard work. Maybe Curtis would know her name or at least something about her."

"My mind keeps going back to how she just came up on us at Hilda's, and she does have a strange look about her."

"Yes, almost like some of my paranoid patients when they stop taking their medicine. Curtis is due early next week. I'll try to catch him. I'll leave a note with his check and ask him to call me. I wonder if that woman knew Hilda. She did live nearby. Maybe we are on to something.

Trish changed the subject. "Prissy you and Reggie seem to have major problems. Do you think there's any hope for you?"

"I'm beginning to think not. If he would stop drinking, there might be a glimmer. We were so in love in high school, and in those early years he wasn't controlling, like now, or maybe I didn't notice. Even Junior has said to me, 'Mama, why does he drink so?' Junior won't even bring his friends over now for fear his daddy might embarrass him. Teenagers are so sensitive."

"Aren't we all?"

"Reggie doesn't think he has a problem."

"We call that 'denial' in the trade."

"I wish you could talk some sense into him."

"Even if I could, I wouldn't, because you're my friend, and I don't see family, friends, or family of my friends, professionally. It's a boundary thing. But, there's a program where the family— that would be Junior and you—and possibly another relation who loves him, or maybe someone he works with who sees how much he drinks, all get together with one or two counselors and bring in the person with the alcohol problem. Sometimes they see the light and agree to get into substance abuse treatment."

"Oh, that sounds wonderful. I wish we could do that. How ever would I get him there?"

"I know a couple of therapists in private practice who

could tell you. I'm not sure, but lots of others have gone before you with similar situations and been successful."

"Would you give me their number?"

"Sure. In the meantime, you and Junior could go to meetings that AA sponsors for family members."

"Could we go even if he is still drinking?"

"Sure. It doesn't matter, and you'll meet some people going through the same thing you all are."

"You're becoming a good friend, Trish. I don't think you realize what it's like to live with an alcoholic, always on constant guard."

"Prissy, that's the first time you've actually said alcoholic about Reggie, and I think that's a step in the right direction. My heart goes out to you. It must be so hard, but you're a strong woman. Give yourself credit."

"Maybe if he stopped drinking, he wouldn't want to do the sex videos."

"Let's hope so."

"I never thought of myself as strong in any sense. I've always let Reggie call the shots, it seems."

"Well, maybe that was the best you could do under the circumstances."

"How much do I owe you for this?"

"Nothing, this is between friends. I'd rather you be my friend than my patient anyway."

❀

TWENTY-THREE

It was the following week when Sheila said, "He's leaving, did you hear?"

"Who, the Chair? I heard."

"No! Dr. Atwater gave in his letter. Private practice in the Houston-Galveston area. At least that's the word. He'll be gone in a week. Can he do that, Dr. Trish?"

"Looks like he's doing it. Someone will have to cut back on their research time to take over his clinical duties and that person will not be a happy camper. Do we have any new faculty in the pipeline?"

"Not that I've heard about."

"The way things are going around here, if several others quit, I might be asked to do inpatient again. Hell will freeze over before I'll go back to that. Maybe I'll take early retirement. If they count the residency years, I'll have twenty in just a couple of years."

"I bet you could make a lot more money in private practice, Dr. Trish. You know so many of the area doctors who would refer to you."

"That probably was the case a few years ago, but with managed care coming in, I doubt it. Now there has to be prior approval for hospitalizations and then for only a certain number of days. So far we haven't worried about it that much, because we get our basic stipend from the university. Then, too, call might be more involved, with no medical students or residents to help out. There are pros and cons to both situations.

"I'm stuck in this area. My parents aren't getting any younger and will be depending on me more and more in the coming years. I guess it's just the way I was brought up. I have medical school classmates living on both coasts who come back once a year or less. I couldn't do that to my family. They wouldn't understand, but would just say, 'Do what's best for you,' then be silently unhappy and lonesome if I did."

"What if you met the love of your life, a soul mate, would you go live in Alaska, say?"

"That might be a different story. I'd have to meet him to know for sure."

"Dr. Trish, you really are a case. Let me know, even if I'm just your secretary. Hell, I might pick up and follow you and let Chris and the kids follow me to wherever."

❁

TWENTY-FOUR

Now, where's that number for Al-Anon? Well, damn! Here it is, right in the phone book. Prissy could have looked it up herself. Well, she'll have to call them herself. This is the best I can do as a friend.

The key—that key Prissy found. I've seen keys like it somewhere else, not used at the medical center, though. It's like a house key, remember? A common type lock.

The next day at the clinic, while chatting with Stan, a social worker, she noticed a clutch of keys on his desk.

"These yours?"

"Sure. Why?"

"Maybe nothing. The one to the office I use doesn't look like these. Are most of the keys to offices in the clinic like these?"

"I think it's a fairly common type and brand of lock, but in a building this old, keys get lost and changed through the years."

"Well, a friend of mine found a key similar to these, in her flower bed of all places, and she doesn't have a clue where it came from. It wasn't to her house. I'll get it and compare it to these. Who knows? But she doesn't know anyone who works here, and these don't look exactly like house keys."

"You're welcome to compare it with mine. See ya around."

TWENTY-FIVE

"Prissy, it's me."

"I recognize your voice by now."

"What's up?"

"Junior is doing well at football. They've won three games straight, a real record for the team."

"About the key—do you still have it?"

"Of course. I even compared it to the keys on Reggie's ring, thinking it might be an extra one to his office. No match there." Prissy continued loading the dishwasher.

"The other day when I was at the clinic, I noticed that someone who works there has keys that resemble your key. The key to my office there is very old. It came with the original building. Apparently some of the locks have been changed over the years, so some of the keys look different. May I borrow it the next time I see you? Have you made that appointment yet?"

"Sure and no, but Junior and I did go to an Al-Anon meeting. Trish, those aren't my kind of people."

"They might not be as well off as you, but I can assure you they are dealing with similar problems, living in a house with an alcoholic. Just keep it up. You don't have to say anything if you don't want. Maybe it would be better for Junior to go to one just for teenagers."

"You're probably right. It's just so hard with his school and football."

"Football will be over by Thanksgiving."

"Sure will. He liked it, by the way, and was happy I recognized his daddy had a drinking problem. He even reminded me that Reggie's dad drank himself to death."

"It's still important to set up that confrontation meeting. The more people who love and care about Reggie, the better it will be. Say, could you drop off that key at my place when you're delivering sandwiches?"

"Where would be a good place to leave it?"

"Put it in a plastic baggie and slide it under the garage door. I don't think it's a good idea to leave it under the door-mat. How's that going, by the way? The business."

"Great! I contacted that policeman's wife, and she wants to help me. She can even do some of the baking—bread and cookies. I'll share the profits with her. We haven't worked out the details yet. She'll come and bake at my house. Says she'll have the bread in pans partially risen, so it will be fresh for that day's run."

"Have you thought of putting a few in some of the Mom and Pop stores around?"

"Yes, only thing is, some of them aren't in safe neighbor-hoods, but we can ask her husband about that. He could probably tell us the areas where the police get fewer calls. Gotta run, bye now. Love you."

"Love you, too."

❧

TWENTY-SIX

Curtis had been early that week, and Trish, running late, had a chance to chat with him in the driveway.

"Curtis, you know most of the folk who do yard work and landscaping?"

"You mean the workers or the outfits?"

"The workers."

"Well, most especially the black people like me. Lately, there have been more of those Vietnam types. They'll do most anything. I don't know their names, usually Dong or Ding or Zong."

"Now, Curtis."

"Dr. Trish, them names be so funny, I don't even try to remember them."

"Any women workers?"

"There're a few Mexican-type ladies I seen around."

"What about white women?"

"Now that is a rare sight. Don't think anyone works regular, like for pay, but there's a volunteer outfit always planting stuff on city and county property, and I seen white women working with them sometimes."

"You wouldn't know any names, would you?"

"No, but Jefferson Paige from church helps out sometimes. Maybe he know a name."

"Do you have his number?"

"No, but it's in the book."

"Okay, thanks Curtis. Gotta run."

"Have a nice day, Dr. Trish."

"You, too."

TWENTY-SEVEN

"Is Mr. Paige in?" It was after dark, Friday, before Trish called.

"Yes? Who's calling?"

"This is Dr. Trish McLeod. I'm a customer of Curtis Blanchard's. He said Mr. Paige might know the name of someone I'm trying to contact." Trish kicked off her shoes and invited Skip up on the sofa.

"All right." The woman's voice, soft and almost musical, called out, "Phone for you, Jefferson."

"Jefferson Paige here, how can I help you?"

"Mr. Paige, Curtis told me you do volunteer garden work sometimes with one of those groups, like the one whose members wear bright green shirts."

"Sure do. Haven't done it in a while, though. Arthritis been acting up."

"Did you ever have a white woman work with you?"

"No, not me, but there was a white lady worked on another team some. Word was she was a strange one. Strong as an ox; used to be real good with the sharp shooter. Dug them holes real quick like. Not much for words, I heard. Didn't visit or chat with the others much. Thought that funny 'cause that's part of the fun of volunteering, the visiting and such."

"Would you know her name?"

"No, but I can find out for you. Give me your number."

"Great! If I'm not here, just leave it on the answering machine."

"Sure thing, Ms. Dr. Trish. Give my regards to Curtis, if you see him."

❀

TWENTY-EIGHT

"How's the homicide investigation going?"

"Which one?"

"The one here, Hilda in the bathtub, the one I can't get off my mind." Clyde was at his usual station when Trish stopped by on the way to her office at the mental health clinic.

"Oh, that one."

"No new leads?"

"Sometimes people brag on the street about what they did, but nothing this time."

"Did they talk to her ex?"

"Yep! Apparently he flew back from Europe and went to the funeral. Still has a fair relationship with some of the family. Whoever slashed her throat was really in a rage, don't you think?"

"For sure, Clyde. Anything else?"

"Yep. They checked some of her VISA receipts from restaurants over the past few months. A couple of the managers recognized her picture. Said she was often with a man— fairly nice looking fellow. Only thing they noticed was he wore his hair slicked back on his head, dark, long but not down on his collar. Always had a jacket and tie on."

"White man?" *Oh my God, could it be who I am thinking it might be?* Trish felt her pulse quicken.

"Yep. Like he was an executive or a professional type."

"And they still don't know his name?"

"Not yet."

"I know someone who wears his hair like that," she said almost to herself.

"Are you sure? I've never seen anyone like they describe. Who is it?"

"Someone at the medical center."

"You should tell the detective on the case."

"I will, but I need to check some things first."

"Dr. Trish! That's the police department's job. If this man you know is involved, it might be dangerous for you."

"Don't worry. I just need to check something, and if he looks like he's the one, I'll call for sure."

Trish could scarcely keep her mind on work at the clinic. Two of the evaluation patients showed up, and she quickly dictated her findings, making a few recommendations for treatment to the social worker who would take the cases, and wrote prescriptions for medications. That finished, she returned the charts and evaluations to the file room.

"Where do you want these, Melissa?"

"Over there on that desk."

"Do you lock up everything each night?"

"Sure do. Every single file has to be under lock and key, tight as a tick, and the door locked. Only the people with master keys can get in here."

"I forget. Who's that?"

"Maintenance and the manager, for sure. The others I don't know, but it's four or five more. I just have a key to this room because it's my work station."

"I was just curious. See you later."

TWENTY-NINE

It was the weekend again before Prissy called. "You won't believe this!"

"Of course I will. What's up?"

"We had the confrontation meeting Thursday night. Reggie is in treatment at the Mont Dieu for thirty days. He didn't get to see Junior's football game, but, heck, he missed all the ones before from drinking or whatever he was doing."

"How'd it go?"

"At first, he was mad as a wet hen and then tears came up in his eyes. It was like he was relieved yet half-sad, half-mad. Junior and I have to go for some family meetings, but that's good. I stopped by before the football game, and he confessed to a lot of things. Like he had been sleeping with other women for years. So many, he couldn't remember them all."

"Oh, Jesus, did you ask your doctor if you had anything when you went for your checkup?"

"I did. She said she didn't think so and did some tests. I got a letter in the mail that said the results were negative."

"Well, that's a relief."

"To be honest with you, Trish, our sex life had eased off, especially after those years when he was so demanding and ugly. He said there was a lot more to tell, and he was scared about something he had been involved with that was possibly illegal. I have no idea what. I'll go see him Sunday after church. Maybe I'll stop by your place later."

"Better make it after five. I'm going sailing with the fellows. Steven seems to be growing on me. I find I just like being around the guy, and he has a terrific sense of humor."

*

THIRTY

Saturday, after returning from the store for a cat food and dog chow run, Trish checked her answering machine to find a message from the judge, asking her to call.

"Neville residence, Mrs. Neville speaking."

"Oh, hi, Ms. Mazie! This is Trish McLeod. Is the judge available? He asked me to call."

"Yes, he is, my dear. I'll get him."

"How you feeling these days, Ms. Mazie?"

"Fair to middling. So kind of you to ask. Just a minute, I'll get him. He's taking his before-lunch catnap."

She shuffled off and it was several minutes before the old man's sonorous voice came over the phone. "Trish, my dear. Thanks ever so for returning my call."

"What's up, your honor?"

"Remember that card I found back in the summer, Notti's?"

"Sure."

"Well, as I recollect, I told you I called and it was just some kind of answering machine, and then disconnected. I couldn't tell much else. Well, I was thinking about it again last week and called the number again. It is still disconnected, so I guess that's the end of that."

"You didn't get a look at the people the day you found the card, did you?"

"No, it was just a glimpse. One might have been a woman in something light blue."

"Well, maybe it wasn't anything after all."

"There's nothing more to do at this time. Stay in touch."

Rub-A-Dub-Dub Death in a Tub 109

"There's nothing more to do at this time. Stay in touch."

THIRTY-ONE

Dinner Saturday was a gathering of three couples at Steven's condo. None of them were associated with the medical field except Trish. Steven cooked.

His townhouse is in the same area as Hilda's. When we go sailing tomorrow, I'll ask him if he ever heard of her.

The sail was fun on Sunday, but neither Steven nor the guys knew Hilda. They had only read what was in the newspaper, and they were unfamiliar with a Notti's.

Back home, Trish had showered, washed her hair, and changed into fresh clothes by the time Prissy arrived.

A towel still on her head, she mumbled, "Just a second. Let me dry this a little."

Prissy sat on the toilet lid watching her.

"Now, let's have something to drink, and let me hear the latest on Reggie. Diet Coke or Diet Pepsi?"

"Diet Coke, please."

Snuggled in her chair, Smoke in her lap, Trish said "Shoot."

"We had a really good, long talk this afternoon, and you'll never believe who he was seeing last spring. Hilda!"

"Hilda, who got her throat slashed?"

"He swears he hadn't seen her since June. She just came on to him like gangbusters and he couldn't help himself. Maybe his mind was clouded with alcohol."

"Must not have been too clouded to get on with it. Where'd they meet?"

"All sorts of places. His office, after hours, her condo," she paused, "and some place over by Pass Christian. It was like a movie studio, but in a condo near where Camillle came on shore. He said one room was like a store with all kinds of sex stuff. Handcuffs, whips, and even dildos. I've only seen pictures of dildos in a book."

"Do you even know what they are, Prissy?"

"I didn't, but Reggie said it was something that two women use for sexual relations. I was just horrified. He said another room was set up to watch movies or videos, with a couple of couches and a bookcase full of videos. Trish, he felt so bad telling me this. Said he had to get it off his chest. But that wasn't all! A third room was set up for video filming; a big bed, cameras, lights, mirrors and all."

"And Reggie went there with Hilda?"

"That's what he said."

"Did he ever see anyone else there?"

"No, he said Hilda had a key. Reggie swears he broke off with Hilda in late May, and she was threatening to tell me about the affair."

"Blackmail?"

"Not a lot, Reggie said, as if that mattered; fifty or a hundred here and there. She'd ask for a loan, but they both knew it wasn't a loan. That's why he was drinking so bad this summer. He said he was terrified the police would suspect him. He swears he didn't kill her. He's sorry he suggested us doing the sex videos."

"What do you think, Prissy? He sure has a temper when someone crosses him."

"I want to believe he's not involved; his previous affairs are already enough to cause a major rift in our marriage. There's no hope if he killed Hilda."

"What if he didn't kill her, but was somehow involved?"

"That's still a big problem for me. I just don't know."

"Do you think that key you found could be to that condo?"

"Reggie said Hilda had a key."

"She could have dropped it in his pocket. If he was drunk,

he wouldn't even notice. Do you think he would tell you the address of the condo in Pass Christian?"

"I don't know. Why?"

"If we knew the address, we could see if the key fits that lock."

"Do you think we should do that?"

"Prissy, if we tell the police about Reggie and Hilda, they'll suspect him for sure. They haven't made much progress on the case so far."

"Okay, I'll ask him tomorrow when I visit."

❋

THIRTY-TWO

The following week, over lunch, Trish quizzed Clare. "What's the scoop on Dr. Ass's departure?"

"Not much. Everything is hush-hush."

"Clare, have you ever seen anybody else wear his hair like Dr. Ass, all slicked back like that?"

"I've seen some characters in movies like that, but no real people around here. Why?"

"Remember how I told you I have some nice chats with Clyde, the police officer, who is usually on security duty when I go to mental health?"

"Yes."

"Well, I was pumping him about how the investigation was going, and he said some VISA receipts were found from a restaurant, and when they questioned the manager, he remembered seeing Hilda several times. And the guy she was with wore his hair slicked back and long. Could it have been our Dr. Ass?"

"Wow! He's a creep, but murder? Actually I wouldn't put anything past him. He's so flat at times, no effect. The couple of murderers I've seen as patients were like that, until they exploded in an unbelievable rage.

If he did, how could they pin it on him, Trish? Maybe DNA evidence?"

"That would work, but give me a break. Our coroner is a smart cookie, but he hardly has money to pay for old-fashioned autopsies, much less routine DNA testing."

"Do you think he collected any samples?"

"I'm sure he did and has just stored them. If they really suspected Atwater, maybe her family would chip in for the DNA testing. Or if it was a strong case, McInnis would come up with the money somehow. When's Atwater leaving?"

"He's gone."

"The ink is hardly dry on his letter. It hasn't been a week since the Chair received it."

"He had annual leave, so he left early. He'll come back to check out with human resources and turn in his keys."

"Did you hear of any friends or associates since we last discussed him?"

"No. I tried to be friendly when he first came, but after the way he acted, all those sexual innuendos and leers, I avoided him. Damn pervert!"

"We don't know he's a pervert for sure."

"Looks like, talks like, acts like, is—that's the way I see it. I'll bet you a dinner that we find out it's true."

"Well, let's define 'pervert.' Maybe he just has a high testosterone level."

"Oh, Trish, really!"

"I mean something like real kinky sex, s-m, bi, tri? Does that make him a pervert?"

"Okay, okay! I get the picture. I still say he's a pervert."

"Do I get to pick the restaurant?"

"Restaurant? You have to cook, Trish."

"All right. And what the hell was he doing eating out with Hilda? There may be more to poor Hilda than anyone realized."

"Whatever are you talking about?"

"Can you keep a secret?"

"You even ask? Of course I can."

"Remember I told you I'd reconnected with an old high school classmate?"

"Yeah, you said she was a real ninny."

"I'm changing my mind about that. She's becoming a good friend."

"Thought you said her husband was a lush, and she was afraid he was about to start slapping her around."

"That's true, but he's in treatment now and, I hope, recovery from his alcoholism. The biggy I wanted to tell you is, he confessed to Priscilla after starting substance abuse treatment that he had been sleeping with Hilda last spring."

"No way!"

"Yep! And Hilda was pulling a little blackmail job on him. He swears to Prissy he didn't kill her, but he's terrified he'll be a suspect if this comes out."

"How does he wear his hair?"

"Lost cause there, Clare. He's losing hair, receding temples.

The tide is going out."

"So maybe it was ol' Dr. A with Hilda."

"She apparently got around. Clyde said the restaurant receipts were for last spring; I'll bet it was him. As the little guy on TV used to say in a German accent, 'Very interesting.'"

❋

THIRTY-THREE

The phone was ringing when Trish arrived home. Dropping two bags of groceries on the kitchen table, she picked up the phone.

"Hello?"

"Trish, I couldn't wait until the weekend to tell you. Reggie gave me the address."

Prissy fluffed her hair and examined her chin in the mirror as she spoke.

"Did you tell him why you wanted it?"

"No. I thought he had enough on his mind now and didn't need to worry about this."

"Okay, can we go over Saturday morning?"

"Sure."

Trish opened the fridge and stashed the veggies in the crisper. *I'll wash them later.*

"Bring an umbrella I think it's supposed to rain, and don't wear anything too bright. We don't want to be too noticeable."

"Oh, boy, now we're acting like private eyes."

"This isn't the movies, Prissy."

"I guess I got a little carried away."

"That's all right. Ten-ish?"

"Sounds good. My car or yours?"

"Yours. My T-Bird is more noticeable."

"Okay, see you then."

❀

THIRTY-FOUR

The overcast sky with its threatening clouds did not help the mood of the women as they made the trip west toward Pass Christian.

"It'll be raining by the time we head back."

"Rain beats snow any day. At least we never have to deal with that. How you feeling?"

"Me? I'm okay, but a little shaky in the mid-section. You?"

"I'm downright scared. What if we open the door and there's someone there? Or worse, two or three someones? We could leave the engine running in the car for a quick getaway."

"Don't be so dramatic."

"There it is, Trish. Let's circle around the back and see if there's a car parked in the slot assigned to it."

"They're numbered. Well, if someone is inside, they didn't park a car back here. Everyone who lives here must work on Saturday or go to the casinos to gamble. There's only one car way down at the other end. Do you want to try the key back here? Bet it's the same lock as out front."

"Good idea! We won't be as obvious."

As they clambered out of the car, Trish opened the gate to the small patio. "Bless Pat. It's been landscaped. It's small, but someone has put in a lot of work. There's even a fountain with a little stream."

"Some of this stuff looks dead to me."

"Must not have been watered in a while. The things out in the open look okay. I guess the rain watered them."

Peeking through the door, Trish said, "It's dark in there. Can't see much."

"Open it, or try to."

"Where's the key?"

"I gave it to you."

"Oh, yeah. It's in my pocket. Voila! Here it is." The key slipped into the lock without difficulty, and Trish started to turn the doorknob.

"Here, Trish, cover the knob with this." Prissy handed her a couple of tissues from her purse.

"Where'd you get that idea?"

"Oh, I just thought, if there's something in there, we might not want anyone to know we were here by leaving finger-prints."

"Aren't you the sleuth? Ready?" Trish turned the knob, pushed the door open, and stepped inside, flipping on the light switch with the tissue. "It's empty!"

"Let's look around. Maybe there's something in another room or upstairs."

"There's nothing up here, either," Trish said, coming down the stairs. "Bare as a baby's bottom."

"I guess this is a dead end. I wonder who owned or rented this?"

"Bet we could find out at the manager's office."

"Might as well." Let's do it."

A small, neat white sign out front marked the manager's office—a front room of another townhouse.

"You go ask."

"No, you."

"We'll go together," said Trish and rang the bell.

"Come in, it's open!" an elderly, gray-haired man called from behind a desk, where he sat watching a football game on the television. "Can I help you?"

"We were wondering who lived at number 1440? We're helping an underprivileged family set up their own home, and we need some plants. Someone told us there might be some at that location that could be donated."

"Let me look it up. Memory's not what it used to be, but I have it here in the computer. Yes, here it is. A.P. Atwater rents it. Rent is paid through next month. Looks like it was paid every three months. Come to think of it, I haven't seen anyone around there in awhile. Used to see cars when I walked the dog in the evening, but not lately."

"Do you have a phone number?"

"Sure, here, I'll write it down for you. Good luck with your project. There's certainly a need for decent homes for the poor. I'm glad I have this place. My kids help with the rent, and I make do with the little salary I get for listening to resident complaints. A while back, 1440's neighbors complained his visitors were parking in their slots. Had to leave a note telling him to have visitors park on the street."

"Did he do it?"

"'Pears he did. Didn't have no more complaints."

Back in the car, Prissy said, "That was a lie about us being on some project like Habitat for Humanity."

"So what? It was all I could come up with on the spur of the moment. Unfortunately, I know about a P. Atwater. Yep, it has to be him. That isn't a common name. It's the fellow I told you about, in my department no less! And he's resigned and left town. At least I won't have to put up with his shit anymore."

"Please Trish, your language. Left town?"

"Yes, he's gone. Left real quick like. No one in the department seems to know why. He never had much to do with folks. A loner type."

"He lived way over here?"

"We don't know that. I probably can worm his address out of Marsha or better yet, get Sheila to nose around."

"Don't tell them too much."

"Don't worry. What do you make of this?"

"I'm mystified. I don't know."

"How'd that key get in your flower bed? Think Reggie dropped it? Since he's in a mood to come clean with you, ask if he ever had a key to the place in Pass Christian where he and Hilda went or a key to her place. He told you she had a key."

"Should I tell him I found the key?"

"Not yet."

When Prissy dropped Trish off, she said, "That was certainly exciting, Trish."

"Really? We didn't find anything and the drive back in that frog-strangling rain was a bitch."

"But isn't it curious? Someone with the same name as one of your fellow faculty members paid the rent."

"Sure is. I have some questions to ask, and I don't want to be too obvious. I'll get back to you. Have a good week."

❋

THIRTY-FIVE

It was Monday evening before Trish called her friend, Barb number two, the toxicologist.

"What's up? Haven't heard from you in awhile."

"Sorry, Barb. I've been busy."

"Have you gotten over seeing that body last summer?"

"Yes, I think so. I had a few weeks of dreaming about it and a startle reflex for several more, but that's mostly gone away."

"A little case of post-traumatic stress, huh?"

"You might say so."

"Say, was that you I saw in a T-Bird? I thought you drove that dusty Explorer?"

"I forgot to tell you. I decided to treat myself to something a little sportier. Steven has a pickup in case I have the need of a truck."

"Cool. You'd better watch out what kind of men start conversations with you now that you are driving a cool, sexy car."

"Now, really, Barb!"

"Just kidding, Trish"

"I know. How's your world?" Trish rubbed Skip's belly with her foot as he rolled on his back for attention.

"Fine. Rocking along. Can't complain. Have a couple of forensic cases in the mill. You?"

"Okay, I guess. Been seeing Steven a little more. Listen, I need to tell you what my friend Prissy and I've been up to. Remember, I told you about the strange key she found in her flower bed, and how we got this wild idea to see if it fit Hilda's condo?"

"Yes, did you all try it?"

"Sure did, but it didn't fit. Well, Prissy asked Reggie the address of the place over in Pass Christian that Hilda had taken him to for some sexual trysts. He, being in a very confessing mood, in treatment and all, told her. We went over Saturday to check it out. The key worked."

"And did Reggie have a key?" Barb stopped doodling and leaned back in her chair.

"We don't know that yet but Prissy is going to ask him. He's really scared someone will find out about Hilda and him, and he'll be a suspect."

"Did you find anything?"

"The place was empty, just drapes left on the windows. We went to the manager, made up a reason to need the name of the tenant. You won't believe in a million years who it was?"

"Surprise me. Is it someone I've heard of on the Coast?"

"More than that, someone you actually knew."

"Knew?"

"Yeah, he's gone now, Dr. Phillip Atwater, former member of the department, himself!"

"Oh my God! Did he live way over there?"

"I'm not sure. I have Sheila checking into the address he gave at school."

"Trish, you need to tell the authorities."

"Not yet. But it sure makes things more interesting."

"Do you think it's the same man?"

"Barb, how many men do you know, or have you ever seen, who wear their hair like he did?"

"Well, none, I guess."

"Point made."

"Gosh, do you think he killed her?"

"I wouldn't put it past him. He was such a cold fish and all that sexual crap he ran on about."

"Didn't he see the patients prior to their sex change surgery?"

"He's the one."

"Did he have anyone like that in therapy when he left?"

"I don't know for sure. He usually had one along. I can check that out at the university clinic where he saw private outpatients."

"Keep me posted."

※

THIRTY-SIX

"Morning, Sheila."

"Morning, Dr. Trish.

"How's your week been so far?"

"Usual. Oh, I got that address for you. Dr. Atwater lived just a mile or so from the medical center."

"Has he been back for any mail?"

"He came last week, checked out through human resources, and gave a post office box in Slidell as a forwarding address."

"Not Houston? Wonder what he's up to now?"

"I'm sure no good. I've told you my view of that creep. Wouldn't want to meet him in a dark alley. He just seemed to be the kind who could really go off if he were pushed."

"I wouldn't know. I was able to avoid him for the most part."

"That was smart of you, Dr. Trish."

✸

THIRTY-SEVEN

"Psychiatry Clinic, Marsha speaking."

"Marsha. This is Dr. Trish. Can you tell me how many individual patients Dr. Atwater was seeing?"

"Not many. Only three or four."

"Do you know if any of them were in the sex change program?"

"One, I think; a real nice lady or man. I mean, he looked like a masculine lady, but hadn't had the surgery as far as I could tell from the chart."

"You read the notes?"

"I just glanced at them when I pulled the chart. They were real short and vague, no juicy details."

"Marsha!"

"Sorry, Dr. Trish."

"Do you happen to remember any other people he was seeing?"

"There was one old lady. She must have been in her seventies; she looked rich. Wore lots of diamond jewelry. She was in for depression. One fellow in his twenties told me he was a musician. He had depression, too. The other one he saw was weird if you ask me."

"Who was that?"

"It was a woman. At least that's the way the chart read. She was very masculine and, funny thing, she always left by way of the back exit. Never walked through the waiting room, and she paid cash."

"Cash?"

"Yes, cash. Not even a check, and I can tell you we're not used to receiving cash. It made more work for me. Actually, she stopped coming back in spring. Let me bring it up on the screen. Yep, last visit was the first week of March."

"Any idea why he was seeing her?"

"Hard to say, those notes were really vague. You couldn't tell what they talked about."

"What kind of diagnosis did he give?"

"A V-Code, I think. Yep, here it is, a Phase of Life problem. Since she paid cash and was his personal patient, it didn't matter what the diagnosis was."

"Does the computer show any prescriptions he might have written?"

"No, it's not in the computer database, but if you'll hold on a minute, I'll pull the chart."

"Thanks, I'll hold."

After several minutes, Marsha returned to the phone. "Here it is, Tommie Sue Brantley. Isn't that interesting? He gave her Prozac and, of all things, Viagra, the sex drug."

"Thanks, Marsha. By the way, what's her address?" Jotting down the address, Trish suddenly realized it was the same street Hilda lived on.

Gosh, I wonder if she knew Hilda. Looks as if another trip for a look-see is the next order of business.

There was no phone number listed in the chart, and when Trish called information, none was listed anywhere nearby, either.

❖

THIRTY-EIGHT

It was Friday night, and Prissy was on the phone.

"Well, this is one week I'm glad is over, Prissy. I covered some clinical duties Dr. Ass usually did. How's your week?" Trish continued gathering clothes and loading the washer.

"I think there's a light at the end of the tunnel for Reggie and me. Trish, I'm beginning to see the real Reggie again. The family meetings are helpful, too. And the sandwich business is booming. Clyde's wife, Susie, is a great help, and she makes excellent bread."

Prissy selected a bottle of mauve fingernail polish and began painting her toenails. *This is multi-tasking. I'm doing it.*

"Good. You'll never believe this, but I decided to check on Dr. A's patients at the clinic. He only had three or four, but one of them lived on the same street as Hilda."

"Oh, yeah?"

"And she stopped seeing him in early March. Also, she paid in cash. Want to drive by the address tomorrow and see how close she lives to Hilda's place?"

"Sure. I feel like Hansel and Gretel, following a trail of crumbs through the forest. Let's hope there's not a witch if we find a gingerbread house. Pick me up around 10:30. I have a few things to do around here first."

❀

On Saturday morning, Trish drove them to Hilda's neighborhood. "There's the number. It's only a couple of doors from Hilda's place. I wonder if she knew Hilda?"

"Do you want to see if she's there and ask her?"

"No. We don't have any official reason."

"Maybe it's time to talk to a professional, someone in law enforcement."

"I'll find out from Clyde who's working the case now, and we can go see him, or her."

"He'll wonder what we've been up to, like going over to Pass Christian. I sure don't want Reggie hurt. What if he's involved more than he's admitting to? After all, he did admit to an affair with Hilda in the spring and going over to the sex club more than once."

"He was probably drunk when he did that."

"Let's hope so, Trish, but that's not an excuse. What about the guy in your department? I'll bet anything he was with Hilda those times in the restaurants. The unusual way he combs his hair is certainly an identifying characteristic, like a tattoo would be."

"Should we drive by?"

"Maybe she'll be outside and we can see what she looks like."

"Okay, but I don't think—bless my soul! There she is, pouring fertilizer or something on those mums by the front door!" Prissy ducked down as they passed by.

"Why'd you do that?"

"I don't know. Reflex, I guess. Did you see her?"

"A little more than I would have liked. She's the one we saw when we tried the key on Hilda's door, strong, masculine looking.

"And what was she seeing Dr. A for? "Marsha said 'phase of life problem.'"

"What's that?"

"It's sort of a benign diagnosis, if you ask me. Just to have something for the record."

"Wonder if she's a gardener like Hilda was?"

"Could be. She sure looks strong and you saw her last summer with the Green Garden Gang, in front of the food stamp office."

"Yes, I did. It was her. I sure didn't like the way she looked at us when we were here before."

"We could talk to the manager of these condos. The manager in Pass Christian was certainly chatty. Maybe this one will be also."

The manager's office, located around a curve at the entrance to the development, was quite similar to the previous one visited.

"Looks like a rubber stamp."

"Maybe it's the same developer."

"I wonder if this manager will be a chatty little old man?"

"You-hoo. Anyone here?"

"How may I help you?" said a silver-blue-haired matron. "Good morning, ma'am we're wondering if you could tell us about 1243."

"It's empty now. Do you want to rent or buy?"

"Rent at first. You see, my friend here has an aunt who's getting up in years. She's still at the old home place over in Alabama. She's not ready for assisted living yet but thinks she wants to be closer to some of her kin."

"She'd be welcome here. There are more than a few seniors in the town homes."

"How are the neighbors around here? She's active and would like folks to chat with?"

"The neighbors on either side work. I don't think they're around much, but there's Ms. Tommie Sue, a couple of doors down. I see her out and about but not lately, come to think of it."

"How come number 1243 is empty?"

"The owner, Hilda Rasberry, died last summer, and it's taken a while to probate the will. Would you like to see it? I have a key."

"Not today, thanks, but we'll call when we do. Did you know the owner?"

"As well as most of the residents. She was in and about, like Tommie Sue. In fact, they were friends. I noticed them planting petunias together last spring and riding bikes together."

"This Tommie Sue, what's she like?"

"She mostly keeps to herself. She's renting, but she doesn't hesitate to complain about the other residents."

"Complain?"

"Oh, the usual, music too loud for her, someone's dog pooping on her grass, or a cat using her flower beds for its personal potty."

"We'd better be running along. Thanks for talking with us."

❁

In the car, Prissy commented, "You sure are getting good at making up lies as you go along. I have an elderly aunt—come on now, Trish."

"I had to think of something. Look who ducked down when we drove by this Tommie Sue's. Wonder how she made her money? If she was seen during the day and at different times doesn't sound as if she has a regular job, does it? But she has money for the rent and had money to pay Dr. Phillip Atwater, at least last spring."

"Do you think she was really his patient or the visits were just a front for something else?"

"Something else?"

"What is your fertile little brain cooking up now, Trish?"

"Nothing. I'm just saying we need to keep an open mind, look outside the box. There's a lot here that just doesn't hang together. Somehow they're all connected, Hilda, Reggie, Dr. Ass, and this Tommie Sue. And we don't know who else. Remember, we're thinking outside the box."

"Well, at least we could have looked at Hilda's place. The old lady has a key and wants to show it. Let's take her up on it."

"Let's change the subject."

"All right. How's your love life these days? Are you and Steven getting serious?"

"Maybe. He is, as they say, growing on me, and I'm not growing any younger. The old biological clock is ticking. What about your love life?"

"It's certainly better now that Reggie isn't drinking. He even says he'll go to church with me, but he wants to pick out another one. We think we'll go visit the Episcopal Church. Try it on for size, so to speak."

"As Dolly, my mama's old maid used to say, 'It's the same Jesus.'"

"That's true, and if Reggie would be more comfortable, I don't mind changing membership."

"What about your old pastor and church friends? How will they take it?"

"They'll be hurt, but they'll get over it. It will take some time."

"I can't believe you're talking this way. Months ago, you'd never have considered a move. Wouldn't want to hurt anybody's feelings."

"Well, they're responsible for their feelings."

"Wow, you're really taking hold of your life, aren't you, Prissy? Shows people can change without therapy."

"I'm simply taking a long, slow time to grow up. My adolescence lasted twenty years longer than need be. But Reggie is changing now, too, and I'm not so sure he would've stayed with me, if I acted the way I do now, back then."

"Say, Prissy, what's your middle name?"

"Helen. Named for my great aunt. Why?"

"I think I'll call you Helen. Prissy doesn't fit you anymore. Helen has a more assertive, powerful sound. So, from now on, you're Helen. How does that grab you?"

"Terrific! I've always felt people talked down to me, never taking me seriously."

"Great! When are we going to look at Hilda's place?"

"You decide, since you work longer hours than me."

"I need a mental health day. How about I take off early Wednesday? We can go after your sandwich run."

"Sounds good."

"I'll call the manager and tell her we'll come by about 2:00 or 2:30."

❁

THIRTY-NINE

The early fall afternoon was pleasant, a little cooler with fewer sun hours. Some of the oppressive summer heat had eased, although even in summer, the Gulf sea breeze made life more tolerable than for the people further inland.

"Here's the key. Should we park in the back or front."

"Let's do the front. We're considering renting or buying, remember?"

"Sure."

"This is interesting. The lock is Baldwin."

"Whatever are you talking about, Trish?"

"Look. See how shiny the brass is, not a hint of tarnish?"

"Maybe it just has lacquer on it?"

"Not Baldwin."

"What makes you such an expert on this? It doesn't say Baldwin on the key."

"On one of my Saturday morning trips to Home Depot, a helpful, handsome hunk told me all about this brand and how it's made to never tarnish."

"So what?"

"It's an expensive lock and I noticed."

Inside now, Helen called from the master bathroom, "Trish, come check this out."

"Wow! She spent a bundle on this, or someone spent a bundle on it. These are very, very expensive fixtures, and look at the size of that tub! I think this is real marble on the floor.

"You should see the kitchen. It's a marvel, too, top of the

line everything. Zero fridge and freezer, even warming drawers like she was a chef/gourmet cook or something."

"These drapes aren't shabby by any means. Very expensive fabric. Look here, Trish. Everything so spotless, except a stain on the carpet here in the bedroom, right by the entrance to the bathroom."

Intrigued, Trish knelt and sniffed. "Helen, I'd swear it's that same funny smell I noticed in the toilet at the clinic."

"Maybe it's some sort of massage oil."

"Everything in here is very expensive, like you'd see in a big three- to four-hundred-thousand-dollar house. Most people who have the money to get this quality wouldn't put it in a townhouse."

"All I can make of it is that she was very well fixed or was associated with someone who was."

"Maybe she got alimony."

"Not enough to afford this."

"She had a husband. Wasn't he an ex who was out of the country when she was killed?"

"He was an ex. Maybe he hired someone to kill her, didn't like paying alimony."

"You've been watching too much late night mystery on TV."

"Nothing more to see here. Let's turn in the key. I need to get home and cook some chickens to make a new batch of chicken salad for the sandwich run."

"You're going to continue once Reggie is sober?"

"Believe it. I love doing it, and it's my ticket to independence, an insurance policy of sorts."

"Keep up the good work." As she dropped off the now-Helen, Trish said, "Maybe we're getting close to talking to the authorities about our suspicions. Think about it."

"Call me over the weekend."

"Count on it."

❀

FORTY

"You aren't ready to talk to the police yet. They'll laugh you out of the room," her toxicologist friend Barb said when Trish told her the latest. Barb continued. "They might not in front of your face, but nothing will come of it. At this point, all you have are a series of things that somehow are related, but you have no idea as to who did it or why."

"Barb, Hilda had a secret life that had to do with our former co-faculty member, Dr. A. What do you think he was up to at that condo? And now he seems to have dropped out of sight. He has Sheila forwarding only first class mail."

"Do you think he was making money over there?"

"He sure didn't use it as an address for school, did he? Ever notice his clothes?"

"Not especially. I had as little as possible to do with him."

"Well, I did. His suits were very expensive. Saw a label once. It was an Armani."

"On his salary? You're sure?"

"Hell, yes! I can read," said Trish.

"I'm just surprised. So, he has an expensive suit. How about his shoes?"

"Murphy and Johnston."

"How could you tell that?"

"He took them off once in a department staff meeting and I noticed the name because Steven has some like them, and they're not cheap. Now mind you, Steven doesn't wear expensive shoes, but he says other shoes hurt his feet and rationalized it was better to get one good pair of dress shoes that last than keep replacing cheap ones."

"My question is, Trish, why are we spending so much energy on analyzing this twerp?"

"Because he knew a murder victim a lot better than you or I or a lot of people did, and he had seemed to have big-time financial resources."

"I think down deep you suspect he killed her."

"You may be right, Barb."

"By the way, did he ever see patients at the mental health clinic like you do?"

"I think he went one afternoon a week, never when I was there."

"Then he was familiar with the place. Did the police question him like they did you?"

"Probably not, since he wasn't there the day the body was discovered. I can check with Clyde on that. Something also happened at the med center that we don't know about. I think he was up to something bad or illegal, whether or not he was involved in Hilda's murder, and they let him resign and move on so that whatever it was never need be made public."

"It wouldn't be the first time the higher ups did something like that. If he made restitution, it would keep administration from admitting to any wrongdoing. It's seen as risk management."

"I remember the residents complaining about his leaving the University clinic early. If he was signing those billing slips without seeing the patient after the residents did, even for a ten minute charge, that could result in big problems."

"There are a couple of others who do that. I don't think that's big enough to result in a forced resignation."

"Say, I have an idea. Suppose that condo Dr. A. rented was a sex club or something. If it were, he could have made lots of money. It's close enough to New Orleans for customers, and maybe the police/sheriff isn't so vigilant about traffic to a condo. Especially if there isn't a history of complaints from the neighbors."

"How could we find out?"

"With your forensic work. Ever have contacts over in Louisiana?"

"Yes indeed."

"Maybe they could ask, like on the street, what was available in the nature of a sex club, more than just prostitution."

"I'll call a lawyer I've worked with in the past. He's a nice guy, but has defended some pretty shady characters in my opinion. Some of them certainly owe him a favor and also would know 'the word' on the street."

"Good deal."

"Trish, are you turning into a sleuth?"

"No, I plan to talk to the authorities fairly soon, I hope. Why do you say that?"

"You're certainly obsessed with this murder, just like you used to be when you had a puzzling therapy patient.

"I'm simply curious about what happened, especially when the connection with the department and Reggie came up."

FORTY-ONE

"It's the weekend, and I'm checking in with you."

Trish told Helen she had asked Barb to see if there was, or had been, word on the streets of a sex club in western Mississippi.

"I wonder if the police have talked with that Tommie Sue woman?" she continued. "A manager saw her with Hilda, and so they may have been friends. She would be able to tell the police some of Hilda's associates at least."

"How's lover boy?"

"Who?"

"Steven, you know who I mean."

"Fine. Well, more than fine. How's Reggie?"

"Seems to be holding his own. He goes to an AA meeting five times a week. That's okay with me, if it keeps him sober."

"I'll ask Clyde next week if they talked to Tommie Sue."

❀

FORTY-TWO

On her next visit to the clinic, Trish made it a point to seek out Clyde for a chat.

"Do you know or could you find out if the detectives have talked with a Tommie Sue Brantley? She may have been a friend of Hilda's.

Trish told Clyde about the visit to Hilda's condo and what the manager shared regarding seeing Hilda and Tommie Sue together last spring.

"You going to be here a while?" he asked. "An hour or two."

"I think I can find out."

❈

Back in his office Clyde called the police station. "How're you doing Jack?"

"Good, what's up Clyde?"

"I have a question about a case. Don't tell that prick, Detective B.S., I called you."

"Which case?"

"The woman found in the bath tub at the mental health clinic."

"Not much activity there since summer. Everyone we questioned denied anything that would show a reason for her death."

"Did you ever question a woman named Tommie Sue Brantley?"

"The name doesn't sound familiar. What's her relationship to the case?"

"Maybe none, but one of our doctors was looking at a townhouse for sale with a friend and it turned out to be Hilda's townhouse. The manager mentioned that Hilda seemed friendly with a neighbor by the name of Tommie Sue Brantley. They rode bikes occasionally and went for walks together."

"I'll check her for you. He'll want to know why."

"Tell him what I just said."

❈

Clyde stuck his head in Trish's open doorway. "Mission completed."

"Great. How about a sex club, Clyde? Do you guys check out stuff like that?"

"Why's a nice lady like you asking about something like that?"

"Just curious."

"I think we'd have heard a rumor if there was one around here."

Trish gathered up her belongings. "I have to get back to the medical center, Clyde. What did your friend say? Walk with me down to my car. We can talk on the way."

"No one has spoken to a Tommie Sue Brantley yet. I suggested that little action, but said not to tell Detective B.S. where the idea surfaced if possible. Jack will handle it."

"Let me know what he says."

❈

FORTY-THREE

A few days later at the medical center, Barb poked her head into Trish's office.

"I've talked to my lawyer friend, Mario, and he called around, pulled in a few paybacks. It appears something of that nature, a sex club, was available; however, his information located it in another area, on the Bonito Chico River. Advertisement and solicitation was by word of mouth, and a phone number guided clients to the semi-secret location. It was very expensive."

"Any name for the place?"

"Yeah, he mentioned 'Notti's.' Ever heard of that?"

"No. Thanks for the info."

I'm getting good at this lying. Time to talk to the judge again.

FORTY-FOUR

"Helen Smithe here."

"That's nice. You're using that name now?"

"I've even asked Reggie to call me that. He's mystified but seems agreeable."

"This weekly phone chat is getting to be a habit, *n'est-ce pas?*"

"Well, if you're bored with me…" Helen fluffed her hair and checked her makeup.

"No way. I've some new information on our case."

"Now we're real detectives."

"I wouldn't quite say that."

"I remember you were going to talk to the authorities and leave it up to them."

"Not yet. Our Tommie Sue person moved out in September, and left no forwarding address. Said she would send one when she found a new place. The manager seemed to think she was moving to Louisiana."

"Did you find out what kind of work she did?"

"That's a mystery, also. Manager told the police she hadn't a clue, but the rent was always paid on time, and she kept the place neat."

"I wonder if she went to the funeral? We could ask one of Hilda's sisters. Or someone in the Garden Club might know. There's a meeting soon. I'll call someone from the yearbook. Wait a second, Trish. Here it is, and there is her number. Lucille's the biggest gossip in the club. I'll call her now. Talk to you later."

❁

"No, I didn't go to the funeral," Lucille told Helen, "I think her sisters took the body to some family cemetery near their home place."

"Would you know any of her sisters' names or phone numbers? I realize it's late, but I thought I'd write a little note. I can call information and get the number. Thanks a bunch, Lucille."

Helen punched in Mary Rennol's number, and a pleasant voice answered.

"I knew poor Hilda from the Garden Club," she told the woman, "and didn't get to the funeral. I know it's been a while, but I want to write a note of condolence to your mother. Did many people come for the funeral?"

"No, it was a graveside service with mostly family."

"Did her friend Tommie Sue come?"

Helen, you lie so smoothly!

"No, Hilda didn't have many friends after the divorce. She became a loner, as far as we knew. She didn't call us often. Her exhusband came, and there was another man there who stood a little ways back. He didn't say much only said that he was a neighbor."

"Do you remember what he looked like?"

"He wore a suit and tie. Fancy looking if you ask me. His hair was slicked back real smooth."

"Thanks for talking to me. I'll get that note off to your mama."

❁

FORTY-FIVE

"Trish? You'll never believe what I found out."

"Sure I will, Helen. Did you call one of her sisters?"

For Trish these frequent phone conferences with Helen highlighted her day and gave her relief from an otherwise hectic pace at the medical center.

"Sure did! And there were only a few people at the funeral. No Tommie Sue or anyone who could have been her. But, there was a man, the sister said, who was a stranger. He told her he was a neighbor."

Helen fluffed her hair and checked her nails. "He dressed real fancy, expensive, and wore his hair slicked back. Now, who do we know who wears expensive suits and keeps his hair slicked back? Your Dr. Ass."

"That's interesting, but if I tell the police, they'll say 'so what?' I have a coffee date with Judge Neville Saturday morning. Want to come? He told me he saw something last summer he thought was suspicious, but nothing came of it. However, he found a business card for Notti's. When he dialed the number, it was disconnected."

"Sure. Maybe he'll remember something more."

"Meet us at Murrell's, 9:30 Saturday."

❁

The early regulars had departed, for the most part, and Trish, the new Helen, and Judge Neville had the place to themselves.

"And who is this lovely lady?" he said when they walked in. "Meet my friend, Helen."

"My pleasure. Have a seat, my dears. And to what do I owe the honor of this meeting?"

"Remember that card you found last summer? It was a sex club over near Pass Christian, but it's closed down now. Do you remember anything more about what you saw from your window that day?"

"It was only a glimpse, mind you, but there appeared to be some sort of conflict, and one party was a woman, I think. They moved around the corner, out of sight."

"What, out of the ordinary, did you observe, judge?"

"A smudge located head high and about two, maybe three, inches across. It looked oily and had a strange odor; however, there was something slightly familiar about it. I've not identified it in my mind to this day."

"Could someone's hair dressing, or oil, have made it?"

"That's certainly a possibility."

"Know anyone who wears that gunk on their hair? A lot of black people do."

"Didn't see enough to say. Like I said, it was just a glimpse."

"Do you know anyone who might tell us about things on the street, from that perspective?"

The judge thought a few seconds and then replied, "Oscar might. He operated the elevator at the hotel. The renovation cancelled the need for his services. We had many a fine chat riding up and down."

"How old is he? As old as you?"

"No, no. He's 20, maybe 30, years younger. He was just a lad when he started. He has his own little grocery store now. I usually stop by every two or three months."

"Will you see what you can find out and get back to me?"

"Certainly, my dear. Possibly we're on to something. At the very least this is entertaining. I find myself bored more often than not these days."

❖

"He certainly has a quaint manner of speech," Helen said later.

"That's his age and upbringing, almost a stereotype of the southern gentleman, but don't let that fool you. He used to party with law students in the French Quarter, even when he was on the bench."

"Appearances can fool me. What next?"

"Who wears thick, greasy stuff on his hair?"

"Dr. Ass?"

"The same."

"Where do we go now?"

"Let's see what Oscar says."

❖

FORTY-SIX

The grocery store, worn with age, but neat and tidy on both the inside and outside, was Oscar's pride and joy.

"Anybody here? Who's minding the store?" The judge raised his voice as he entered. Oscar appeared from behind an upright cooler.

"Sure 'nuff. Well, your honor, what you doin' down here? Slumming?"

"Hardly."

"Good to see you anyways. Cup of coffee?"

Mugs in hand they sat in two old squeaky, cane bottom straight chairs, the padding of which showed years of use.

"Oscar, ever heard of a sex club on the Coast?"

"What? Now, judge you know me better than that."

"Just thought you might have heard some hoochie-mama type customers talking."

"Well, I do have a few lady customers that I suspect might be hoochie-mamas, but I ain't heard nothing 'bout no sex club."

"I'm not sure there is one. Just a rumor I was asked to check on."

"Folks come in this store ain't got money 'nuff for that, even

if they might want to."

"How's the family?"

"Jist fine. Got a boy in college, wants to be a teacher. Everybody doing fine. Yourself, judge?"

"Fair, I guess. The wife's health is failing, mostly just old age with me."

"Good of you to stop by. Sorry, couldn't be more help."

❅

FORTY-SEVEN

"Helen, the judge's friend didn't know anything helpful. Do you think Reggie could show us the place he and Hilda went?"

"I'm not sure, Trish. He feels bad about that, especially now that he's sober and going to church and all."

"Would you ask him anyway? If it's the townhouse we can be sure it was a sex club."

"I'll get back to you later."

Trish's phone rang at 9:30. She closed the book she was reading.

"The chickens are cooling for tomorrow's salad, and since I talked to Reggie tonight, I wanted to give you a report."

"Shoot. What did you find out?"

"He says he was always so drunk he wouldn't be able to find it. He only had an address. Hilda did most of the driving. He said that sometimes there were some black women and men there. Saw them in the room where the 'sex toys,' as Hilda called them, were for sale. Sometimes, Hilda wanted him to do stuff to hurt her. Said it turned her on."

"Did he do it?"

"He said he hit her a few times with a whip, but just lightly."

"Oh, God!"

"He was remorseful when he told me. Said he had prayed for forgiveness and that it was behind him now. Says he's been 'washed in the blood and is now clean.'"

"Boy! That's Baptist apostolic, not Episcopal talk."

"I think he went to service with an AA buddy, but we joined the Episcopal Church."

"Did he say anything else?"

"Only that Hilda hinted she might be bisexual and how a ménage a´ trois might be fun."

"Jesus! This gets worse. Did he?"

"No. Said he drew the line."

"Know who the other woman would have been?"

"No, but I think when he realized she was engaging in homosexual relations, that's part of what turned him off, drunk or not." Helen felt tears come into her eyes.

"More important, how are you dealing with this information, Helen?" Trish sat on the side of the bed and leaned over as she talked.

"I suppose a part of me would rather not know; however, I'm giving him a chance, since he's staying sober and talking to me and Junior. It's as if the real man is emerging from some horrible bondage. He'll be discharged in another week. Well, my chickens are cool, gotta run!"

❈

Driving to the medical school the next day, Trish went over the previous night's conversation with Helen.

Wow! Our little Hilda had a secret life. Wonder if her homosexual interests played a part in the breakup of her marriage? Wonder if she had a lesbian lover? Was she screwing Dr. A.? They were seen together on several occasions and it's pretty sure he was paying for the sex club condo.

'Where More is not Enough.' That's what was written on that business card the judge found. Would Dr. A. engage in a ménage a´ trois? I wouldn't put it past him to do anything. It's about time for me to call the authorities and unload all this.

Later that afternoon a knock at her door awoke Trish from a vertical catnap.

"Come in, the door's open."

"Dr. McLeod?"

"Dr. Trish, please."

The detective entered and took the offered seat. "The office said you had requested an interview and might have some information on a homicide case?"

Trish related what she thought pertinent, leaving out that Reggie had any relationship with Hilda. Detective Bill Swanson, a taciturn fellow in the same blue blazer, stupid yellow tie and khaki slacks, politely took notes.

"Anything else, doctor?"

"No. How's the investigation going? It's been several months now."

"Well, we knew about Notti's, but by the time it was checked out, the place was empty. It also seems Ms. Hilda made frequent trips to New Orleans and the West Coast, maybe twice a month, and led an expensive lifestyle. Clothes and jewelry in her townhouse indicated that unless she sold jewelry and clothes from her home, her cash flow was significant. Didn't appear she was in debt, either. Contact with her family was minimal after her divorce a couple of years ago. Her ex added nothing to what we already knew.

"What is it about you psychiatrists? Here I am telling you all this, when my job is to hear it from you."

Trish smiled. "I suppose we just have a way of inviting people to talk."

"We'll talk to this ex-faculty member. Do you have an address or phone number?"

"No, he told the department he was going into a private practice situation near New Orleans, but in that event, there ought to be a listing with Bellsouth."

Trish thought, as she escorted the detective from the department, *This is the guy who Clyde hates and who gives him such grief. He sure was on good behavior today. Butter would have melted in his mouth.*

❊

FORTY-EIGHT

On the phone that night, Trish told Helen what had transpired. "He was nice, kind of preppy looking with a blazer and the same yellow tie he wore last summer. He was pleasant and professional. Didn't tell me much, but the police suspected a sex club, and Hilda had plenty of money. She must have been getting income from the club. Maybe she and Dr. A. were partners. You think?" Trish continued folding a load of clothes as she talked.

"Possibly. I keep going back to your Dr. A."

"He's not my Dr. A. We just worked at the same place."

"He's disappeared now, for all practical purposes."

"That's true. At least now the police can put some sort of tracer on him. To change the subject, remember your telling me about the people in the green shirts outside the food stamp office?"

"The Green Garden Gang, they call themselves."

"You'll never believe who's joined them. Clare, my friend in the department. I introduced you to her a while back when we ran into each other at Wal-Mart, remember?"

"She was friendly and nice looking, and I liked her hair color. I wonder if she knows that Tommie Sue woman? There was a gal who looked a lot like her in that group when I saw them. Remember I told you?"

"I'll ask her. This is a new activity for her. She wasn't a member until just recently. Tommie Sue left town in September."

"I think you should pump your policeman friend, Clyde. That detective didn't really tell you much."

"Okay, but I don't think Clyde knows a lot."

"Listen, I bet those guys talk just like we do, especially when an unsolved homicide is involved."

"I'll ask. Maybe they're overlooking something. You're working with Clyde's wife now on the chicken salad run. Ask her. Maybe she's heard something."

"It's not just the chicken salad run now, Trish. I'll have you know we've evolved to ham, Italian meatball, and tuna fish sandwiches, but I'll ask her."

"Swell. See you later."

FORTY-NINE

"Dr. Trish, you sure are interested in this Hilda case," Clyde noted as they drank coffee together, the result of yet another patient not showing up for an appointment.

"It certainly is a mystery. Have you heard anything else on the side that seems odd?"

"They said two women admitted going into that toilet the morning the body was discovered, but there were only two sets of recent fingerprints. Yours weren't there."

"I can explain that. The cleaning crew went over everything the evening before so there would be only prints from that morning, and I didn't leave any prints."

"How so?"

"Well, I wash my hands the way infection control says—take a paper towel to turn on the water, toss that towel in the trash, wash my hands, take another paper towel, and use it to dry my hands, then turn the water off, and use the paper towel to open the door. Toss that paper towel in the first trash container I come to."

"That's quite a ritual."

"One can prevent picking up infections that way. Were there any prints on the toilet flush levers?"

"Only those two sets."

"That's because I trip it with my foot. Listen, Clyde, will you let me know if you all find out where Dr. Atwater has relocated? He might not have gone to Louisiana after all. I think from something he said that he was licensed in several states—Louisiana, Texas, New Mexico, and Nevada.

"And can you tell me if a trace is being run on the Tommie Sue gal? They both left town near the same time. I just found out a colleague of mine has joined the Green Garden Gang. Maybe she can find out something about Tommie Sue. I've already discovered it was Tommie Sue my friend Helen saw with them in front of the food stamp office. Maybe it will be a good idea to see exactly when and where the Green Garden Gang has had public gardening or landscaping projects."

That night, while scanning Christmas catalogues that piled up like leaves in autumn, and fighting off Smoke's advances, she answered the phone to hear the pleasant voice of a Green Garden Gang member.

"Dr. McLeod. I'm Doll Strain from the Green Garden Gang. I had a message on my answering machine. Are you interested in joining us? We have a wonderful group."

"I'm not sure. Can you tell me a little about what you do?"

"Well, we're a strictly volunteer, non-profit organization. We plant flowers, trees, and shrubs on public grounds. Mostly we just plant and the city or whatever agency is responsible for the upkeep. We don't edge or mow grass or stuff like that."

"Where have you done projects?"

"Oh, on several streets with a wide median, the food stamps office, the post office, the library, and the mental health clinic to name a few."

"How do you decide where to go?"

"Usually someone, like a manager, calls and requests that we beautify an area."

"Did you have a member by the name of Tommie Sue Brantley?"

"Sure, Tommie Sue was a real good volunteer, strong as an ox. She really helped a lot when there was heavy work to do. She's not with us anymore, moved away late last summer."

"Do you know where?"

"She didn't say. In fact, she never said much of anything. Aloof, if you ask me. We all tried to be her friend, but she wouldn't even sit and have a Coke when we took a break.

Stayed to herself, but what a worker. Most of us didn't work the late afternoons, having families to fix supper for. We'd work some on Saturdays, and in the summer we'd try to work only in the mornings. A couple of times, when we had to leave, she stayed on, even after the office or building closed. She sometimes got the cleaning crews to let her in, if necessary. Some places have their own equipment, fertilizer and all, and she'd put it away."

"Do you ever have a key to the places you work?"

"No, never."

"Can you tell me anything else about Tommie Sue?"

"Well, just that she was moody, and the way she handled that shovel she seemed angry a lot of the time, but she wanted to work and we needed the man—I mean woman power."

"Thanks for calling back."

"Sure thing. If you're looking for a nice community activity, we'd be glad for you to join us."

Not in your lifetime, I don't like to sweat, Trish thought as she said goodbye and replaced the phone.

"Well, Smoke. What do you think of that? I guess I'll call a few managers—the food stamp office, the post office—and I can ask Tillie at the clinic who has keys. It's strange, Smoke, isn't it? Tommie Sue was Dr. A.'s patient at the university clinic, and we think they both left town about the same time."

❋

Tillie's office door was always open, and since Trish had another 'no show,' she took the opportunity for a brief chat.

"How are you doing, Dr. Trish?"

"Okay, I guess. I'm not quite over seeing that poor woman in the tub last summer."

"I'd have that thing removed, but the powers that be say we don't have the money this year. It must have been awful for you, seeing the body and all?"

"It's not something I want to repeat, I can assure you. Tillie, who has keys to the building and the alarm?"

"You want a key, Dr. Trish?"

"No, just curious."

"Well, I do, some of the section supervisors, the medical director, and the maintenance man, Brian."

"What about the janitorial service?"

"Yes, they do, but not the actual workers. Their supervisor has a key and is responsible for locking up and re-setting the alarm."

"What time do they finish and lock up usually?"

"Around 8:00 or 8:30 p.m., but never later than 9:00."

"What time in the morning is the building opened?"

"Brian gets here about 7:00 to 7:15 and opens up, turns off the alarm and turns on the lights."

"Is Brian around today? We have good chats every now and then."

"He's probably in his little office by the boiler room. He has a beeper, so I'll have him come over."

The boiler room was located in a small building adjacent to the main building, so it was a few minutes before Brian stuck his head into Trish's office.

"What can I do you for, Dr. Trish? Long time no see. How ya'll are?"

"Hi, Brian. Do you know of anyone who might have keys to the building, other than people who work here?"

"Well, come to think of it, I did lend one last winter to them gardening people who planted them memorial trees."

"Did they return the keys?"

"I'm not sure. Oh, my, don't tell Ms. Tillie! I'd be in hot water for sure. They wuz more interested in what time the building was opened and closed, and I plumb forgot 'bout that extra set."

"What happened?"

"They wuz going to work on a Saturday and wanted to

put the fertilizer and tools that belong to us back in the stor-age room under the building."

"Remember who you gave the keys to?"

"Not 'xactly, a nice white lady, real sweet."

"Would you mind checking if they've been returned?"

"No problem. Used to hang them on a hook by my desk, as I have a set to myself."

Later, as she walked to her car, Brian hailed her. "They is back, Dr. Trish. Please don't mention it to Ms. Tillie."

"Sure thing, Brian."

I wonder if Hilda or Tommie Sue worked on the plantings last winter? Since Clare has joined the Green Garden Gang, maybe she can find out.

Checks with the food stamp office and post office revealed no new information. Both places said their security guards who came by periodically would have opened the building after hours for someone from the garden group.

❁

That evening as she picked up clutter and loaded the dish-washer Trish called Clare.

"Hi it's me. Remember you told me you joined this garden thing? Could you ask if they know or remember who planted flowers and trees last winter or spring at the mental health clinic?"

"I'll ask around. Who are you curious about?"

"Our murder victim and Tommie Sue Brantley."

❁

FIFTY

"Anybody home?" Helen called out from the front door.

"Sure, here I am, taking out the garbage. Come on in and take a load off your feet. Any news on our great mystery?"

"Clyde's wife told me they found out Dr. Atwater worked a couple of weeks in Nevada, a locum tenens tour."

"Yes, the post office had forwarded mail, and he was contacted by phone. Sheila just told me."

"When was that?"

"Back in September. And he told the school he was relocating to the New Orleans area."

"Is he still in Nevada?"

"If he is, he's not doing locum tenens or medicine now."

"Did the police go out there?"

"No. They just talked to him on the phone. Dr. Atwater said he knew Hilda as an acquaintance. Had dinner a couple of times, and he didn't consider her a friend."

"Yeah, I really believe that," Helen replied sarcastically. "How'd Clyde know?"

"He asked around. Those guys are a bunch of old biddies when there's an open case like this. I talked to Clare to see if there were any records, or if anyone remembered who planted flowers last winter at the clinic. Seems Hilda and Tommie Sue both helped."

"I don't suppose she asked if the two of them were on the same team?"

"She did and they weren't, as far as anyone could remember or the records showed. They keep cards on each team to track the number of hours of service."

"Can you think of anything else we can do now?"

"It's time for another conversation with Judge Neville. He's a smart old codger. Maybe he can figure out what happened. How's Reggie and Junior?"

"Fine. Reggie is still, as they say 'in recovery.' Goes to a lot of his AA meetings. Junior and I go to our meetings about every two weeks now. This fall will be a lot more pleasant than last year, that's for sure."

FIFTY-ONE

The judge's suite on the top floor of the hotel was a step back into the early fifties, except for the new TV set. Several barrister-type bookcases with glass fronts lined one wall of the sitting room. Trish checked out a few titles, not all law books. In fact, the variety was remarkable. The old man read well, from Shakespeare to James Joyce, to ornithology and even theology, with a translation of some Karl Barth.

"Please take a chair, my dear. So glad you graced me with a visit. Tea? Cookie?"

"Yes, please."

"So, what's new?" the judge said as he prepared tea at the small Pullman kitchen adjacent to the sitting room.

"Not much, unfortunately. Where's Ms. Mazie?"

"She's visiting her niece up near Meridian for a few days. I'm glad she's feeling a little better. Any arraignments on the murder case you were telling me about?"

"Not so far. What are your thoughts, judge?"

"Well, my dear, it was a crime of passion, that's for sure."

"Did I tell you she was probably unconscious when placed in the tub, with the back of her head smashed in pretty bad?"

"So, she was in the tub, probably close to death anyway, when her throat was slit?"

"Looks that way. By the way, any further thoughts on what you observed last summer?"

"Some. I agree with you that the oily smudge was hair dressing, which was left when he, or she, was shoved or pushed against the wall. Not exactly a fight, just a shove, because it was so quick."

"Think it had anything to do with the Notti's card?"

"Possibly. You say both Dr. Atwater and this Tommie Sue woman have disappeared? And that Dr. A. was seeing the victim last spring?"

"Well, he denied it was anything other than a casual dinner or two."

"And this Tommie Sue was a patient of Dr. Atwater's at your university clinic?"

"Yes, that's what the records show."

"So, how'd the body get in that bathtub?"

"Someone dragged or carried her into the building after hours, sometime during the night."

"Do you think one person could do that?"

"If they were strong, especially since Hilda was slight in build."

"Two would make it more feasible."

"The police questioned everyone at the clinic the day the body was found. Thank goodness I was one of the first. There must have been fifty or sixty people, including the patients, there that day. I went back to school, not that I got much work done. They also later questioned some of the people who live nearby. There are some houses about a half block away, behind the clinic. One said the dogs were barking furiously about one a.m."

"Could the body have been dumped without anyone seeing?"

"At that time of night and in that neighborhood? Sure. And if they had keys, the alarm wouldn't go off. The maintenance man admitted he loaned a spare set of keys to the Green Garden Gang last winter, and they're now back on the hook by his desk."

"I don't believe they will get an indictment on this case without a confession from the killer."

"That doesn't look likely. Do you think there's any connection with the murder and what you observed last summer?"

"We'll never know unless we talk to one of the persons I saw, and that's not likely, is it? Why did Hilda's friend, Tommie Sue, leave town?"

Trish shrugged. "Tommie Sue was an aloof, loner type."

"You said she was rather masculine, appeared very strong. Could she have frequented the sex club?"

"I think folk who run that sort of establishment prefer it to be called an adult entertainment club. Of course that's from reading, not actual experience. But sure, she could have used it. Some shy, introverted people with very poor interpersonal skills and high sex drive would gravitate to such a club."

"Was it a bordello?"

"In a sense. There certainly was sexual activity going on there; however, they also sold videos, and sex paraphernalia and made referrals."

"Referrals?"

"My friend's spouse, who went there a couple of times roaring drunk, doesn't remember much. But the town house isn't that large, and if a customer wanted a particular sexual service or experience for a fee, they were referred to another location."

"Did they take credit cards?"

"I think he said they did."

"That would be a way to check on the volume of business."

"Great idea, judge! The police would have to do that. I'll ask my friend Clyde."

"Well, at the least, it would appear that this Tommie Sue woman and your Dr. Atwater—"

"He's not my friend, judge. We just worked in the same department."

"Anyway, they were somehow involved."

"The police don't know where Tommie Sue is, and they already questioned Dr. A. about his relationship with Hilda.

They didn't bring him back from Nevada, so he must have an airtight alibi."

"It would appear that door is closed. Hilda didn't bash in the back of her own head, get into the bathtub, and slit her own throat."

"To be sure, judge. As we discover more of her secret life, we know she came in contact with more than one weirdo, and this adult club must have handled a large cash flow."

"Then one must consider organized crime's involvement."

"I had my friend Barb ask her contact about that. Mario is over in Louisiana. He said the word on the street was that a sex club was available somewhere in the area. He didn't have any details. Need to ask him about any criminal connections."

"The Big Easy Clan has a finger in almost everything shady, even in these parts."

FIFTY-TWO

Back at the office a note from Clare that read, "Want a trip?" gave Trish a good excuse for an early break.

"What's up, Clare?"

"Oh, I'm going to the American Group. They're having it in Las Vegas in a couple of weeks. Wanna be my roomie? Sam refuses to go to Vegas."

"I thought it was later, like in February in New York or on the West Coast?"

"Used to be, but now they're spreading it out and trying some different times of the year."

"I'm not doing group now."

"Do you still pay your dues?"

"The department does, so I would qualify for a discount on the hotel."

"Think about it, Trish. You need a break. You're the least-traveled person around this place. What's the latest on your sleuthing ?"

"I've told the police all I suspect. They have no leads either. Hilda apparently had a number of rough contacts in her business, if you can call it that. Barb's friend Mario said it was almost certainly the mob. They had at least a part interest in the sex club; however, it has melted away, and no other has formed, or if so, it's underground."

"So, it's a good time for you to get away. You haven't been anywhere since summer."

"I'll think about it."

"Well, it's always a fun meeting, as meetings go. This

group knows how to laugh and party and not be analyzing everyone. If you don't want to party, it'll be fun to watch the rest of us. You can even gamble a little."

"Giving my money away is not my idea of fun."

"You might win something."

"No way, I've read how the casinos work."

"At least it will be a good place to people watch, and there are some great shows and restaurants."

Glancing at the meeting dates on the sheet Clare handed her, Trish added, "That's the weekend Steven has a business trip."

"Oh? How's 'Mr. Lovey,' your personal, helpful, handsome hunk?"

Smiling, Trish replied, "Just great. Think I'll keep him around awhile."

"Is that a blush I see on the face of Miss 'I'm never going to get involved with a man again'?"

"Maybe."

"Oh, you two cooking something up?"

"I'll let you know. By the way, do you snore?"

"Sam says I do a little, but not bad. You'd better decide today and let Sheila know, so she can make your plane reservations. Don't forget to get prior approval. Time is short."

"Okay, I'll go with you."

"Great! I'll call the hotel and tell them to give us a room with two king-sized beds."

❀

FIFTY-THREE

"Now, that wasn't a bad trip, was it?" Clare plopped down on a large bed in their hotel room.

"Wow! This is pretty nice and a great price!"

"They make their money from the gaming tables."

"So, I'm just part of the overhead. We can at least walk through and look at the place later."

"Your wish is my desire. Lead the way."

After, passing rows of zombie, glassy-eyed patrons of the machines, Trish said, "Boy, that's a real downer in there."

"What do you mean?"

"Clare, didn't you see those players? Talk about a negative energy drain. That place is a black hole if ever I've felt one."

"Most of them didn't look too happy. The ones who play the card games appeared to be happier."

"I doubt it, but it wouldn't take much to be happier than those poor bastards."

"Well, bless my soul!" said a voice beside them. "Is this who I think it is? Trish McLeod? And lovely Dr. Clare?"

"Oh my God!" Trish whispered under her breath. "Phillip Atwater with bushy hair?"

"Indeed it is. How are you, ladies?"

"Fine, thanks. What are you doing here?"

"Attending the conference. I've relocated in the area, did some locum tenens work. You know, no overhead. Say, let's have a drink together. I've got to run now, but could we meet, say fourish, in the Stardust Lounge?"

"Sure," piped Trish.

"Great! See you then."

"I don't believe it!" Clare hissed. "You actually accepted an invitation to be in his presence, after all those months, even years, of avoiding him back home? Are you out of your mind?"

"No, I want to hear about his relationship with Hilda."

"I suppose you'll say, 'How many positions did you use? Have you memorized the *Kama Sutra?*'"

"Not like that, Clare. I just want to hear what he says when I introduce the subject."

"I wouldn't miss this for the world!"

"He invited both of us. You avoided him just as much as I did. He certainly looks different without the slicked down hair. Now he looks more normal and, did you notice, no sexual innuendos."

"Our meeting was rather brief."

"We both know that Phillip never required time to put forth that kind of garbage. It rolled out of his mouth like water off a duck's back. I noticed he appears thinner and the expression around his eyes has changed."

"I thought you never looked at him long enough to see his expression. And what's with this Phillip stuff, Trish? Going soft on the guy?"

"I'm not sure. He somehow seemed different."

It was four on the dot when Phillip Atwater, already seated, arose to greet them as they came to the small table and chairs in a corner of the lounge.

"So good to see you two. What can I get you to drink?"

"I'll have a white wine," said Clare.

"Chardonnay, okay? And you, Trish?"

"Diet Coke."

"Oh, now, this is Vegas. Live a little!"

"If you insist, I'll have white wine since Clare's having one."

"I'll have the same," Phillip said to the waiter, a handsome, clean-cut young man. "So, how are things back at Harvard on the Gulf?"

"Now, really, that's not kind. It's about the same, people come and go."

Phillip replied quietly, "And people die."

"Yes. We heard you were questioned concerning Hilda Rasberry's death."

"How'd you know that?"

"Clyde, my friend who does security at the mental health clinic told me, since I saw her body in the tub."

"Well, they called me out here a while back, since I was a friend. The week of her death, I was visiting the only relative I have a relationship with, my younger sister Ruth, up in St. Joseph, Montana."

The waiter served the wine and as Trish took a sip, she said, "I have to ask this. Are you the real Phillip Atwater? Not one single sexual joke or comment spoken in fifteen minutes.

"Look, Phillip, I'll cut to the chase. I have nothing to lose. You might have been at your sister's; however, I have information that tells me you were involved in some shady business down on the Gulf, a sex club of sorts. Was that an outgrowth of your 'sexual research?'"

"Trish, don't be so hard!" Clare placed her hand on Trish's arm.

Phillip looked downcast. "It's all right, Clare. I deserve it. Trish is right. We're all shrinks here and can analyze each other 'til the cows come home, but that doesn't change reality. Look, I loved Hilda. Yes, I know, you two would find it hard to believe, narcissist that I am—hopefully now a recovering narcissist. However, even though she was as deep as I into the sex club, somehow we found each other. I know how corny it sounds to a couple of hen psychiatrists but for the first time in my life, and hers, too, I think we shared unconditional love for each other.

"We both made a lot of money from the club, even after a cut was given to some people in New Orleans. I mean a lot of money. I don't have to work unless I choose to now. Hilda had the adult entertainment venue going when I arrived on the Coast. Her marriage was breaking up, and she was separated. At first it was just a business arrangement for both of us, and because of her divorce, we put the condo/townhouse under my name. I behaved in a clandestine manner so it didn't appear I was doing anything out of the ordinary. There was plenty of business from New Orleans, especially from the convention trade and during carnival.

"Then, last spring, we began to have more than a business relationship. I'm not saying either of us wasn't having quite a bit of immoral sexual activity before that. Immoral, that's a word I didn't recognize back then. Hedonist that I was, nothing was immoral. I now think it was a miracle. God personally intervened in our lives."

"I don't believe this!" Clare exclaimed. "Phillip Atwater saying the word 'God' and not in vain!"

"Look, Clare, we wouldn't have become psychiatrists if at least a part of us didn't believe people can change. I'll admit that part of me was rather embryonic and underdeveloped."

"Look, Phil…may I call you that?"

"Sure, may I call you Trish?"

"Sure. I'm still very suspicious of you. However, you look different, and your speech is certainly clean and not vulgar, as I remembered you. You're sure this isn't another smoke screen?"

"You're certainly entitled to that view."

"We both know a leopard can't change his spots."

"Maybe so, Trish, but there are spots, and then there are other kinds of spots. You're looking at a man who had over three hundred hours on the couch before he went south to the Gulf. I pretty much knew what I was, but I had no desire to change my lifestyle."

"Have you gone religious?"

"Not exactly, Clare. I know you probably won't believe this, but I was christened as an infant and confirmed as a child. I won't bore you with my crummy childhood. That's for my therapist and me. We all three know, and have read about, people with impoverished and cruel childhoods who are happy, productive citizens, so I'm beyond making excuses.

"Something different and wonderful happened between Hilda and me. Both of us began to regret our previous lifestyles. I'm not saying we were feeling guilt. There was a little of that, but more a realization that the choices we were making didn't result in happiness or fulfillment.

"Yes, we had plenty of money, and Hilda had expensive tastes. Shortly before she died, I remember she revealed that closing doors on that life wasn't as easy as she had anticipated. She didn't elaborate. As for me, I merely composed my letter of resignation and had it ready for the medical school. I'd love to continue this conversation, but I have a seminar now. How about dinner?"

Trish hesitated, "Uh, let me check the conference schedule. I've hardly had time to see what's on it for tonight. Call us. We're here at MGM, say 6:30, after your lecture, and we'll let you know."

"Sure thing. I hope we can spend some time together."

❁

FIFTY-FOUR

Back in the room, Trish and Clare were still in a state of shock.

"Can you believe that guy, Trish? I'm still not sure. Anti-socials can be very charming. Just because he's not overtly talking like before, I'm not ready to trust him."

"The TV shows say there's organized crime operating here. Why is he in Vegas and not Texas or one of the other four or five states he had a medical license for? We could ask him over dinner."

"We can be assertive and leave the table if he starts anything. We're calling the shots this time. He seems to want to talk to us. We can grill him, put him on the hot seat, and gauge his reaction."

"Okay, Clare. You tell him a time if he calls. I'm going to slip into the back of the hall to hear a speaker I've read about and catch the last part of his speech."

"That's you, Trish. Always feeling the need to attend every lecture at these meetings."

"It's my work ethic."

"Ha! My work ethic at present is a short nap! I'll catch the phone if Dr. Phil calls. I think we can call him that now."

"I'll be back around 6:45, unless I meet a helpful, handsome hunk who asks me to have a drink with him."

"Poor Steven."

"Just kidding, nothing serious."

"Let's hope not! It would be a shame to let a catch like ol'

Steven slip through the web you're weaving, even if you don't know it."

"Oh, yeah?"

"Your subconscious is weaving it."

"Yes, ma'am, Ms. Analyst. Sometimes it's a real drag to be good friends with such a sharp shrink."

"Get out of here, I want to take a nap."

"Just a whiff of Bal al Versailles cologne, and I'll leave you to enter sleep and Stage 2 dreamland."

FIFTY-FIVE

The unicorn was smiling, a wreath of flowers around its neck as it stood in the forest glade.

"You're not very big are you? May I pet you?"

The unicorn lowered his head, and as Clare reached to stroke his soft white coat, the jarring ring of the phone returned her to another reality.

Damn! she thought, as she reached for it. Always happens with interesting archetypal dreams.

"Oh, hi, Phillip. Yes, Trish and I talked. She's at a lecture right now, but we'd love to have dinner with you tomorrow. Six-thirty in the lobby? Fine."

Later, during the nightly facial ritual of cleanser, toner, eye cream, and moisturizer, Trish said, "I still don't trust him."

"You have a great gut intuition going for you. More times than not, it's the forecaster for where the action is while doing psychotherapy."

"This isn't doing psychotherapy, Clare. However, I'll share with you my gut/heart reaction to the conversation today. It wasn't the total negative turn-off always present every time I was around him for more than two minutes. Maybe a leopard can change some of its spots."

"We'll get a better picture of that tomorrow night."

"Clare, if you wake me up snoring, I'm getting up out of my luxurious bed and giving you a shove!"

"I'll try to sleep on my stomach. Sam says I hardly snore in that position. Well, good night. Don't let the bed bugs bite."

"God forbid!"

FIFTY-SIX

"Have an interesting day, Clare?"

"Yes. Heard a couple of good speakers, and the small groups are always fun. How was yours?"

"A lively day. Kept busy and met some new people.

"This group isn't quite as uptight as our usual conference members."

"I think so, too," Clare said, as they waited for Phillip and enjoyed the ambiance of the decor.

"Here comes Prince Valiant!"

"Where'd you come up with that, Trish?"

"Hell, I don't know. It's not a permanent label yet."

"Hello, ladies."

"Hi, Phillip. How's tricks?"

"I'm not into that anymore, remember?"

"Sorry. I didn't mean it that way."

"Six months ago, that would have been the appropriate greeting to use. I hope and pray it never fits me again. And, yes, certain elements, or associates, I guess you'd call them, in New Orleans were very unhappy when we pulled out. We were a sort of 'cash cow.'"

"So there was a nice cash flow from Notti's?"

"How did you know the name of the club, Trish?"

"An old friend from my childhood found a card on the street and was puzzled by it. Then, another friend's spouse admitted to her that he had been there with your Hilda last spring. Were those 'associates' in New Orleans so upset that they would do something about your pulling out?"

"At first, I was afraid they might, but there will be another fool to take my place. It just may take awhile. I wasn't that big of a fish."

"By the way, what's your HIV status?" Clare chimed in. "Clare, that isn't polite!"

"That's okay, Trish. I'm negative. Both Hilda and I were very careful about that, and I knew she was HIV positive."

"Looks like she had an active sex life before you."

"I'm sure that was true. Please, let's change the subject."

"So, you're not practicing now?"

"No. When I first left the Gulf Coast, I did a couple of locum tenens jobs, just one or two weeks at a time. When I look back on it, I was in a dissociative state a lot of the time those first two or three months after Hilda died. It was the shock of her death."

"Could you have killed her in a dissociative state and not remember?"

"You don't waste any time, do you, Trish?"

"I don't mean to be unkind, but frankly, we can hardly believe the changes in you. Maybe this is a dissociative state we're seeing right now."

"It isn't, and I can fully understand your suspicions. I told you. At the time Hilda was killed, I was visiting my sister in Montana."

"And that wasn't a usual thing for you."

"No. I hadn't seen her for years and needed some information from her about our awful Catholic childhood. I'm a couple of years younger, and my memories were somewhat spotty. I needed to know what she remembered and also have some closure and forgiveness from her for the way I treated her. Usually it's the older sib who leans on the younger, but that wasn't the case with us."

"Was your childhood why you chose psychiatry, to figure yourself out?"

"Partly. More of us than you would expect choose the specialty for that reason. But, for me, it was also an intellectual curiosity regarding the mind and body connection."

"So, you returned to the coast to find Hilda dead?"

"Yes, I read it in the paper. Ours was a secret relationship— just the two of us, which I realized wasn't normal. We had no circle of friends for get-togethers, just the people we met in the business. Hilda had some activities, like her Garden Club, but they didn't know about me."

"We sure didn't at the medical school. We thought you a weird, introverted, schizoid personality with a hefty dose of narcissism."

"That's a pretty accurate description of the way I behaved. I never met Hilda's sisters or mother. In fact, she didn't have much contact with them either. I felt compelled to attend the graveside services. I really needed that for closure. I stood in the back, not speaking to anyone, and said I was a casual friend when I paid my respects to her family."

"When did you change your appearance?"

"That was after I came to Vegas and gave up practicing medicine. I really needed to straighten myself out, and I had plenty of income from investments I had made when the money was flowing. So, now I'm in therapy with a wonderful man."

"Psychiatrist? Analyst?"

"Neither. He started out as an ordained minister in a mainline protestant denomination, later took a Ph.D. in Psychology from Western Psych, and settled in Vegas."

"Is this a religious thing with you or what?"

"There certainly is a spiritual element, and I believe Hilda and I were soulmates. I know, as well as you both do, that I'm not anywhere near permanently living this change. From my own work as a therapist, I told my patients that two years of practicing the new behavior is minimum for it to, so to speak, become engrafted, and then there would be lapses into the old ways. That happens. Especially when the environmental stress builds up, and I've only begun in therapy. Harry Brown is a terrific therapist."

"Are you ladies ready to order? The calamari is excellent."

Surveying the menu, Trish said, "at these prices all my *per diem* will cover is a bowl of soup."

"How well I remember. Please, my treat. Order what you will. I can afford it now."

"You're on, Phillip," replied Clare and proceeded to order a steak.

"What about those 300 hours on the couch with an analyst?"

"I learned a lot but made no changes."

"The police talked to you?"

"I talked to a detective on the phone and told him what I knew about Hilda's associates, which was actually quite scant. She was killed only a few days after we came to the realization that our lifestyle and the business weren't for us. I went to visit my sister the day after Hilda and I discussed our plans for the future."

"I don't suppose the word, or thought, of it being sinful ever crossed your mind?" Clare, obviously agitated interjected.

"Clare, do you think we should go there?" Trish admonished. "That's all right, Trish. Not at that time, Clare. Neither of us had any religious affiliation or membership, although Hilda came from a very strict and rigid rural 'holiness in God' background."

"'Holiness in God?' I'm not even sure what that is."

"I gather it was a Pentecostal sect. Her father died young from the effects of alcohol. That, too, was a mystery, the strict rigid religion, and yet he drank himself to death. He also abused all the girls sexually, not intercourse, but molestation. Hilda couldn't tolerate the hypocrisy and escaped as soon as possible. Her poor husband was just a front for her activities. Hilda engaged in all sorts of sexual activities for years before our paths crossed, sometimes for free, sometimes for money. She'd been doing the sex club scene for about five years. Her ex, the poor guy, never suspected a thing, probably because he traveled frequently with his work."

"Wouldn't this stuff set the Garden Club ladies on their little pink ears?"

"Please, for Hilda's memory I'd rather they never knew."

"Don't worry, it'll never come from us, our lips are sealed. Right, Trish?"

"Sure, lips sealed."

"I can understand why the police suspected me, but, I wasn't in town, as I told you, and my sister and brother-in-law spoke up for me."

"I can say, Phillip, I certainly suspected you."

"Trish, I remember how you avoided me, and now I have a great admiration for you for not putting up with my obnoxious behavior. You, too, Clare. I didn't bump into you as much, but both of you steered clear, that's for sure."

"So, Hilda didn't have any friends other than you?"

"Not really 'friends,' mainly acquaintances. She talked to a few ladies in her Garden Club and the people who volunteered for the Green Garden Gang."

"Did she mention a Tommie Sue Brantley?"

"No, but she was a patient of mine at the outpatient psych clinic. Where'd you hear about her?"

"I talked to the manager of Hilda's townhouse complex. Tommie Sue was a neighbor of Hilda's, and they were seen going on walks and riding bikes together last spring. I thought if she was a friend, she might know Hilda's associates or friends. I didn't know she was such a loner. Then, the next thing I knew, Tommie Sue up and moved before I could contact her. No forwarding address or anything."

"Phillip, you said Hilda wasn't one to really trust anyone, kept her relationships superficial."

"That's right, Clare, she said that until, to her surprise, we fell in love."

"Frankly, Phillip," added Trish, I'm surprised too. You were a real jerk."

"That was a cover up, a way to prevent anyone from knowing me. Of course, a year ago, I couldn't even admit that was a possibility. Therapy, with a really good therapist, is a good thing."

"Not to interrupt, Phil, but this salad is too beautiful to eat."

"Do your best, Trish, it's only vegies in Sunday clothes."

"What about all the credit card receipts from the club?"

"She kept those, Trish. Most business transactions were cash, and Hilda did the deposits."

"Did you pay your taxes?"

"Yes, that's one honest thing I did, and let me tell you, it was a bundle."

"Where did you tell the feds the money came from?"

"I said it was from consulting fees."

"When you closed the club, what happened to those records?"

"I don't know. Hilda took them away before she was killed. There weren't any in the place when I closed it up."

"What happened to all the furniture and equipment, if you can call it that?"

"A large truck came from somewhere in Louisiana, I'm not sure where, and loaded it up and took it away."

"Back to Tommie Sue. What were you seeing Tommie Sue for?"

"I'm not sure if I should reveal that. She was a patient."

"Oh, wow! After all this other stuff, you're Dr. Upright and can't talk about a patient to another psychiatrist? What did she look like? I think Helen and I saw her when we tried a key at Hilda's townhouse."

"What are you talking about?"

"Helen, my friend, found this key in her flower bed. Her husband had been seeing your Hilda last spring, and we thought the key might be to her place. As it turned out, it was to the sex club. Hilda had taken him there. Anyway, the day we tried the key, there was a rather strange woman out in front of a townhouse a couple of doors away. She walked over, gave us a hard look, and asked if she could help us. She had dark blonde hair and was very stocky, what I call a strong peasant look."

"That's Tommie Sue. I didn't realize she lived that close to Hilda."

"Are you sure she didn't work for you guys?"

"Well, possibly. Hilda could have hired her and I wouldn't necessarily have known about it. If we made a referral for an outside job, she might have had Tommie Sue handle it.

"The most frequent request was for a sexual service performed in a public or semi-public place."

"Like what?"

"Oh, in a car in a public parking lot or on a street corner, someplace that had the potential of discovery. Made it more exciting for the customer. There are some strange sexual practices out there. I'm sure you gals have heard a few from your patients, even if they were only fantasizing about them."

Clare said, "Most of the people I've seen, didn't come to enough sessions for that sort of material to emerge. They were too blocked and defended to reveal that kind of information early on, before secure therapeutic alliance developed. If they did, I'd suspect it was an effort to fake me out. Of course, not on purpose."

"How long did you see Tommie Sue?"

"About a year, Trish, and then she just stopped, no explanation given."

"You aren't seeing her now, Phillip. You never answered my question."

"It was depression. Also, she was a lesbian and unfulfilled in that role. Never found a significant other."

Clare added, "It's been my experience that the gay people we see as patients frequently have personality disorders. The gay people who are our friends and associates, not in therapy, are like the rest of us, just a different sexual orientation."

"It probably took a lot of effort to keep that part of their lives private, especially in the South, outside of New Orleans and the other big cities."

"Back to Tommie Sue," Trish said, turning the conversation back to the subject in which she was interested. "Did she have a personality disorder also?"

"Yes. She never made it in life. In fact, she believed she was a man. So, she was actually transsexual rather than a lesbian."

"Did she want surgery?"

"She had no ovaries or uterus when I began seeing her, at least that's the history she gave. I didn't examine her."

"Maybe it should be 'he.' Since she wasn't a lesbian after all."

"Yes, 'he' was evolving. She was taking testosterone, and the next step was breast reduction, actually removal, but she didn't have the cash to do that when I saw her."

"What kind of work did she do?"

"That was a surprise, considering all her mental problems. She was a licensed physical therapist and worked for home health agencies, but never long with the same one. She'd work with stroke victims in their homes. She was an angry, paranoid person, but not psychotic, at least not while I was seeing her."

"Physical therapists make pretty good money, yet you say she didn't have the cash for the next surgery?"

"That part wasn't clear. Therapy was exceedingly tedious and snail slow. Maybe that was a motive to work for the adult entertainment club, saving money toward her surgery."

"Or she was supporting a *kith of kin* up some hollow in the Smokies."

"Or maybe she was a gambler. There sure was enough temptation around the area, with all the casinos."

"That might explain the cash problem."

"But she never mentioned anything in that regard."

"And Hilda never mentioned a friendship with Tommie Sue?"

"No, never. Maybe, from Hilda's point of view, there was

no relationship other than just another person in her circle of acquaintances."

"Did you ever consider that Hilda was leading you on? Remember the saying, 'Love is blind.'"

"Anything is possible, and I've certainly had that thought since her death. Did I really know her? Whatever the reality, at least a positive result is that I'm getting my head together. Don't get me wrong, I fully realize my personal healing has just begun. With this therapist, I hope to truly evolve into the person I was meant to be. Even if it takes several years."

"Which we know it will, or should, if it's valid," said Trish. "As a therapist yourself, Phillip, you're aware that as you approach the real nitty gritty, Mr. Doubt will creep in and attempt to sabotage you."

"Sure thing, but remember, that money, or lack of it, will not be an obstacle. I have sufficient income from my investments to pay for therapy and live a modest lifestyle here in Nevada. I can always do a week or two of locum tenens work that's near enough to fly back or to drive back for my sessions."

"Sounds great. A part of me still doesn't believe this great turnaround, so be sure to contact me in a year or two for a progress report, or hopefully, a final report."

"So," said Clare, "it would appear that Hilda and Tommie Sue were at least friendly enough to go on walks together and bike rides. A person doesn't usually do that with casual acquaintances, at least not on a regular basis."

Trish continued, "Hilda is turning out not to be the squeaky clean master gardener belle, getting over a bad marriage. Sorry, Phil. I know this is hard for you."

Phil replied, "As I said, we were both, to put it mildly, amoral and hedonistic, but I thought we'd turned a page to another way."

"Maybe you did, but we don't really know about Hilda, do we? Did you two split your share of the income from the club?" asked Trish.

"I thought we did. I didn't really check that closely. It

seemed like a lot for my share, so I was satisfied, and we had such great times together sexually."

"Oh, give me a break!" Clare broke in. "Your testosterone level rose."

"You two gals really know how to lay it on the line, don't you?"

"You asked for it, Phillip. What I'm saying is not from a vindictive position, desiring you to suffer guilt, but rather to point out reality and assist you in your quest for a new life."

"Life certainly has an added dimension now, a spiritual one, not that I've gone religious or that I'm ready to enter a monastery, mind you. Maybe we were touched by an angel."

"We can't be sure of Hilda, can we?"

"I'll grant you that now, but I still believe in my gut that I'm a changed and changing man. But who killed Hilda?"

"I was betting on you for a while there. But now I'm thinking Tommie Sue might be the killer. Phil, you had her in therapy. Is she capable of murder? How many sessions did you have?"

"As I remember, only twenty-five or thirty she wasn't regular. We were just getting started when she stopped coming. I really shouldn't be telling all this, confidentiality and all."

"Come on, Phil. We're discussing a horrid, violent death."

"I guess it's all right. As I remember she had quite a lot of repressed rage. In childhood, she liked to kill animals, and she viewed people as objects. Although she never mentioned a name, shortly before she quit, she spoke of a romantic relationship with a woman and expressed the thought that she might be falling in love. But I can tell you, she would be a jealous type, and I had serious doubts about the love part. Also, this was after starting the testosterone."

"Think Hilda was the object of her affection?"

"That was about the time Hilda and I were deepening our relationship."

"Maybe Hilda was playing both sides of the street."

"Maybe so. A couple of times she alluded to what fun a

ménage a´ trois would be. But in June, she told me she was really becoming committed to me and our relationship. She said she was losing her taste for club activities."

The meal ended with crème brûlée and decaf coffee.

"Well, gang, I think this will continue as an open case for quite a while, unless Tommie Sue is questioned. I don't see much any of us can explore at the present," concluded Trish.

"Phillip, I wish you the best. You have our e-mail addresses too. Stay in touch," added Clare.

"Ya'll, too. Let me know if they arrest anyone for Hilda's death."

"Sure thing."

❀

"Well, that was interesting," said Trish as she and Clare watched Phillip leave the restaurant. He even said ya'll.

"You won't believe what came to my mind at the end of that."

"What?"

"Oh, I thought of the lines from Macbeth, 'When shall we three meet again? In thunder, lightning or in rain? When the hurly burly's done."

"That was three women and witches to boot. I don't think it fits us exactly."

"Maybe the hurly burly, will be done when next we have another discussion with Phillip."

"Let's hope so. Do you think he's for real?"

"That was our second talk with him, and I'm more convinced he is making an effort. Only time will tell."

❀

FIFTY-SEVEN

"So, it's to be a spring wedding? Trish, I'm so happy for you!"

"Thanks, Helen."

"What made you take the leap? That's a lovely ring. A Thanksgiving present?"

"It's just a part of it, a physical representation of us."

"Impressive. Was it a ticket to let him get in your pants?"

"Helen, don't be ugly. Of course not. There are some people in this world who do not just hop into bed at the drop of a hat."

"Not many, I'm afraid. Trish, you're blushing!"

"Am not!"

"Yes, you are. I think that's cute. Where's the honeymoon going to be?"

"Maybe a few days in the Caymans. They're close, and we both like to dive and snorkel, and Steven can sail. I have something to ask you, Helen, formerly Prissy, will you be my attendant?"

"Oh, wow! I'm really touched. Sure you don't want an older friend?"

"Older in what sense? We're about the same age."

"I meant time wise. It seems our friendship only started last summer."

"I always suspected what a great gal you were, even if our paths seldom crossed before last year. How's the business going these days?"

"Great, simply great! I'll make upwards of twenty grand this year. And that's just six months after starting."

"Must be that terrific, addicting chicken salad you make. Next thing I hear, you'll be the second woman to join Rotary."

"Funny you should say that. One of Reggie's business associates wants to sponsor me. We think maybe next year, if the business continues to be successful. At least our personal lives are satisfactory, even if our venture into sleuthing has proved naught."

"I wouldn't say that yet. We gave the police some leads to check on. Our conversation with Phillip jogged my memory regarding a murder several years ago in which a faculty member was suspected."

"I remember reading about it in the paper. A Dr. Ramirez wasn't it?"

"Yes, that's the case."

"Did you know him, Trish?"

"Not well, just to nod to in the halls, and we sat on a few committees together."

"They never had a trial, did they?"

"No, the grand jury didn't return an indictment."

"Do you think he did it, Trish?"

"I could believe it. Dr. Ramirez was a strange one. I never interviewed him or had a real conversation with him, but there was coldness in his eyes. Their blue-gray hue gave him a washed-out look, and he had a serious Roman, hooked nose. He moved with smooth, quick steps like a snake slithering along, and his eyes darted."

"Did his tongue dart out, too?"

"No, Helen," laughing, Trish replied, "but come to think of it, he licked his lips a lot, and he had a nasty way of clearing his throat."

"Do you think anyone from the medical school was involved in Hilda's death?"

"It doesn't look that way at present. The only connection

is that the psychiatry department sends faculty to the mental health clinic, where she was found, a couple of days a week."

"Did any of them have a key?"

"No, I asked about that. The only possible lead or connection was Phillip Atwater."

"You're calling him by his first name now, Trish, not Dr. Ass." Helen straightened her monogrammed apron, adjusted her bra straps, and looked at Trish expectantly.

"It's just amazing, the change in that man. There we were, Clare and I, who have spent more time than we ought analyzing him in the past, and he turns up, nice haircut, clean-shaven, wearing cross-trainer Reeboks, Dockers, and a Polo golf shirt. He even looked fit, as if he were working out or doing some kind of exercise. I forgot to ask him about that. Unless he's a super actor and has covered his tracks, there's no trail there. I tend to believe him."

"Would this Dr. Ramirez be the kind to frequent a sex club, do you think?" asked Helen.

"Probably so. He was such a jerk. I can't see him having a relationship with a woman that he hadn't paid money for."

"Back to the wedding. If you're having a small ceremony, how about a nice, medium-sized reception?"

"That's a possibility, I don't want you fretting over it and wanting to do the food. You're my matron of honor, so we'll hire 'The Upper Crust' to cater the whole affair, and Julia Ripple is the best floral designer on the coast. She owes me a favor for advising her about a nephew in Atlanta who needed psychiatric treatment."

"They catered the last wedding reception I attended. The food was out of sight!"

"I'm getting hungry now."

"Be sure to get some of their onion sandwiches. I know it sounds gross, but they're fab. I'm glad they have a good business and don't want to sell sandwiches to construction workers. I'd like to keep a corner on that market."

"You've convinced me. It'll be fun."

"Any possibility you might do it sooner? Say, during carnival? Mardi Gras is in February, and we could do purple, green, and gold, Mardi Gras colors."

"Don't get carried away, Helen. You're relapsing into belleism."

"What?"

"Yes, back to all that Southern belle crap."

"Well, even if I've changed, I'll never wear white shoes before Easter or after Labor Day. That's just too tacky."

"Oh, Helen, what a case you are. Love ya, anyway. I'll talk to Steven. Maybe we can move the date up."

FIFTY-EIGHT

Sheila had her boxes of Christmas decorations scattered around the office.

"It's a little early for this, isn't it?"

"I need to go through and see if I anything is missing. It's only a few days until December."

"Have you had time to check on those meetings that Dr. Ramirez may have attended?"

"Sure thing. Beth Longnails, in Medicine, was able to find out. She's one of my best sources of dirt…I mean information. There was an ASPET meeting in New Orleans last June. Our former faculty member, Dr. Ramirez, presented a paper."

"No kidding?"

"How do you like them apples?"

"Very interesting. Since you're so up on medical center gossip, Sheila, remember when he was questioned after that post doc fellow in his department was found stabbed to death? What was the gossip then? The grand jury never indicted him or anyone else, remember?"

"Sure, it was all the talk for a while around here, especially among support staff. The consensus was about half and half. Half thought he did it and half not."

"Did his Chair ask him to leave, or was it his idea?"

"Betty said it was his idea. He told his chairman he had an opportunity to do research and not have so much clinical responsibility."

"I'll bet the students and residents breathed a sigh of

relief at that. Even I heard how much they detested him. If there were an award for least liked prof, he would have won hands down."

"Good riddance to bad rubbish, I say. But there's probably another one just like him incubating, slowly gathering strength to emerge as the new, most-hated professor. The funny thing about Ramirez was that it wasn't just the poor or average students who disliked him. The brains and gunners hated him, too. So, Dr. Trish, why are you interested in whether Dr. Ramirez has been back in the area?"

"It may be nothing, Sheila, but he was so weird. He may have been a compensated paranoid disorder for all we know, and he worked in the same department as a woman who was stabbed to death."

"Ramirez. That's a Spanish name, isn't it? I wonder if he had any kin in the New Orleans mob?"

"My understanding is that it's not a mob in the true sense, like elsewhere."

"Yes, but in the papers they talk about Sepulvado and Serrio. Those are Spanish names."

"I think you're grasping at straws, Sheila."

"I prefer to call it thinking outside the box."

"I don't know where to go with this. I'll just tell my policeman friend, Clyde, and leave it at that. I have a wedding to plan."

"Wedding? Oh, Dr. Trish, are you and your Steven going to tie the knot?"

"Yes indeed! At first, we thought March when the azaleas bloom, but now we're thinking Mardi Gras."

"I know your mama and dad will be so happy."

"For sure. A Southern mother can hardly tolerate an unmarried daughter, even if she agreed that the first time was a mistake from the git-go. Now she'll be wanting a grandchild to spoil."

"Are you ready for that, Dr. Trish, at your age?"

"I'm only forty-two, Sheila. Lots of women have babies in their forties these days."

"Well, don't wait too long. Does your mama know yet?"

"Oh, yes, and it's been like a slug of speed for her. Talk about diarrhea of the mouth. She can't stop planning. I may have to get Clare to put her on lithium. Not really, Sheila."

"Will I be invited, Dr. Trish?"

"Need you ask? We're having a large reception, but the wedding will be just for immediate family in the chapel."

FIFTY-NINE

Trish asked Clare to cover Friday and Monday of the long weekend she was going to Key West with Steven. She readily agreed.

"Gee, Trish, you've covered so many times for me when the kids were sick that I need to play catch-up."

"It's not for sure yet. Steven may have trouble getting a place this late."

They were waiting for the chairman to start the monthly faculty meeting.

"Ever notice the group process in these meetings?"

"Well, not exactly, except we always manage to sit to one side and against the wall, never at the table."

The table had always fascinated Trish with its series of drawers along each side—four per side. Once, she had explored the contents. *Might find some money, she mused, as she shifted the assorted pads of paper, stickums, agendas from previous meetings.*

"What in the world? Look what I found. Mint-flavored condoms."

"No way!" exclaimed Clare. "Let me see. Now what are those doing in here? Say, this is the kind they have in the restrooms at the mental health clinic."

"Who do you think put them here?"

"Beats me. They could have been in there for years. As many times as I've been in this room, I've never see anyone open one of these drawers before."

"Someone has. Sheila keeps the schedule of when this room is in use and by whom. I might just have a look at it."

"You are the nosiest person sometimes, Trish."

"Well, it keeps life interesting."

It was 1:30 when the meeting ended, and Trish decided to follow up on the mint condoms she'd found earlier. She checked with Sheila.

"Here's a message from your Steven to call if you have time. He also said he was able to make a reservation."

"Good deal, Sheila. Say, don't you keep a log of who uses the Chairman's Conference Room?"

"Sure do. Reservations are made downstairs where all the rooms are listed." Reaching for the reservation book, Sheila continued, "Here you go…for the last five years. Is that good enough?"

"Sure, I just want to look over it."

"What's up, Dr. Trish?"

"Nothing. I'll tell you if I find anything interesting. By the way, is the room locked at 5 p.m. and on weekends?"

"Sure. Only the master key will open it."

Trish sat at her desk and flipped through the log. Over the past year or two it had not been scheduled for a 4 or 5 p.m. use, except two days a week, and that appeared to have been for medical student small groups or resident lectures.

Oh, what's this? Dr. Ramirez from Medicine scheduled a Friday, 4:15, twice a month, for six months. I wonder if that was when he left town?

Returning the log to Sheila, she said, "When does housekeeping start their evening work, like picking up trash, stuff like that?"

"Mostly, they start about 5:30 when the offices are empty, but not on Fridays. They wait until Saturday. Something about it being cheaper and not having to pay shift differential for night work."

"Thanks, Sheila."

SIXTY

The weather, as it sometimes is in late November and December, was perfect as the plane touched down in Key West, with rainy, cool weather not predicted for a week. Picking up the rental car and a local map, Trish and Steven stopped by a grocery store for supplies on the way to their lodgings.

"I've chartered a little Catalina 25 if you want to go for a sail tomorrow, or I can crew with a guy I met last year on his Erickson 35."

"I'll take you up on the sail. It'll be a good time to test my sea bands to protect me from sea sickness."

"Great!" Steven was familiar with Key West, having made the trip down many times over the years with friends and family alike. "Would you like me to get someone to crew with us? I can call John. I think he has a teenage son."

"Sure. I'm not that good on the lines, and I'd feel more secure with another person on board."

"No problem. We'll come back in for lunch at one of the local hot spots."

After an uneventful, smooth morning sail Trish said, "I think I got a little sun in spite of the sunscreen."

"You look wonderful to me."

"Charmer. That was a nice morning. Nothing like a pleasant sail to clear the cobwebs," Trish mused, as they lingered over a lazy lunch of conch chowder, salad with roasted yellow and green peppers, and fresh baked rolls.

"There seem to be quite a few elderly folk around here,"

remarked Trish, as ancient men rolled by in wheelchairs pushed by attendants.

"Quite a few snowbirds around after November first. Some of them migrate North for the summer, but a fair number live here all year. Not as concentrated as other parts of South Florida, however.

"I saw a couple of interesting shops down the block. Care to escort me while I check them out?"

"Sure. What're you buying?"

"I should get a little something for Helen, Sheila, Barb, and Clare."

She knew Steven was a man who decided, for the most part, what he needed to buy before entering a store and purchased just that item. The idea of looking at merchandise for entertainment was beyond him. However, she was glad he was more than willing to accompany her, especially after he noted a couple of umbrellas with chairs outside.

An hour or so later, Trish emerged with a small sack.

"It took you two hours to buy that?" asked Steven. "Let me see."

"Oh, it's just a few refrigerator magnets made of sea shells."

"Heck, you can buy those at home."

"It's the thought that counts. Actually, the shop was more like a museum with some very fine artwork. Mostly seascapes, water colors, and some nice pottery pieces, all made by local artists."

"You resisted?"

"Well, I might come back before we leave," Trish replied as she replaced her sunglasses that were pushed into her hair.

She lowered her head, took Steven's arm and whispered, "See that man getting into that silver Rolls across the street? I'd swear that's Dr. Ramirez."

"Who's he?"

Trish related the difficulties encountered by Dr. Ramirez when he was on the faculty back home.

"I wonder what he's doing down here?"

"He's probably on a weekend like us."

"He's driving a Rolls, and that's not the usual rental car. Let's go back to the condo. I want to see if there's a Ramirez in the phone book."

"Why? You want to invite him for dinner?"

"No way! I can't stand the guy. I thought he had relocated up North."

At the condo, Steven said, "I'm going down by the pool to read. Care to join me?"

"In a bit. I want to check the phone book first."

"Take your time."

"Here it is. 'Ramirez, MD-PhD, Internal Medicine.' Isn't that interesting? He's left academic medicine, and after all that talk about doing further cocaine research and having less clinical work."

The remainder of the weekend was a welcome respite from the hectic, busy activities of the medical center, and Trish remarked how refreshed she felt as they boarded the plane the following Monday.

"I think I'm ready to plan our wedding."

"I'm glad it will be simple. Can I just wear my navy blue suit?"

"Of course. I'm going to buy a nice dress, maybe a silk cocktail suit. However, that will necessitate a shopping trip to New Orleans."

"I'm sure you can handle that."

"I'll get Helen to go with me. I hope she can get away for a day, now that she's expanded her lunch business."

❀

SIXTY-ONE

Later that day, on the phone for their weekly chat date, Helen agreed to accompany Trish to New Orleans the following week for a wedding dress.

Clare stopped in Trish's office the next day. "How was the long weekend?"

"Great! I feel refreshed."

"You need to be for the next several months. February isn't that far away."

"Clare, you'll never believe who I spied in Key West. Dr. Ramirez! He was even listed in the phone book under Internal Medicine."

"I bet there are enough old codgers to keep him busy down there."

"Yes, but I thought he relocated so he could do research, and now he's in private practice?"

"Stranger things have happened. By the way, I've been thinking about our little chat with Phillip. He didn't tell us much about Tommie Sue Brantley, as far as what was going on at the time he was seeing her. And we know she was at least an associate of Hilda's, and he said Hilda was the love of his life. There might be some connection there."

"He said he didn't know Hilda knew Tommie Sue."

"There might have been a lot of things he didn't know about Hilda."

"Clyde said Tommie Sue had dropped from sight. They even ran her social security number, retrieved from the records at the Psych Clinic, and there has been no activity since last June."

"She could be working freelance and not reporting her income, and if she were a careful driver, there would be no traffic violations," said Clare as she sat on top of the journals in the recliner.

"We know she/he was a physical therapist, and who do they work with mostly? A lot of stroke victims. And who has CVAs? Old people, and where are there lots of old people? All over. But where is there a concentration of *rich*, old people? Florida and a smaller number in Arizona."

"The police really should talk to Tommie Sue."

"But maybe she's already made the switch and is living as a man. She/he could get a fake driver's license and a social security number, for that matter. That's probably not hard to do either, in Florida or Arizona."

"I don't suppose the police have her fingerprints?"

"Not that Clyde knew of, but that reminds me, he told me there were no unaccounted for prints in the area where the body was found. The killer must have worn gloves. I think a call to Phillip Atwater is in order. A conference call with you, Clare."

"What are we going to ask him?"

"More about his patient, Tommie Sue. Do you know any-one in Vegas, like a mental health professional?"

"Yes, Beverly Box. She took some Gestalt training with me back a few years ago. We hit it off as friends, but I haven't kept in touch, except a Christmas card every year."

"Would you feel okay about calling her?"

"Sure. Why, Trish?"

"Perhaps she knows someone associated with Phillip's therapist, or who knows Phillip, and could tell us if what we saw and heard is for real. I think that's very important to know, and then we can ask Phillip some more about Tommie Sue."

"Will do, Trish. First, I'll call Beverly Box, and then I'll call Phillip and set up a time for a conference call one night this week."

"Call me after you talk to Beverly."

"It may take a few days. I'll look her up first online and email her, and then it'll be a few more days until I call. How much should I tell her?"

"Let's do a conference call with her also. It would be better to talk to Beverly first."

❁

SIXTY-TWO

"Hi, Trish. I called the Upper Crust and everything is set for the reception on the Saturday before Mardi Gras. Have you reserved the church?"

"Yes, Helen, and the Parish Hall."

"Are we still sleuthing Hilda's death?"

"Not much these days. My friend at school, Clare, set up a call to Vegas and we chatted with an associate of hers, Beverly Box, who's a therapist there. From what she told us, Phillip's therapist is considered one of the best in the area, and Phillip isn't practicing medicine. I'm still not totally convinced.

"The next night we called Phillip and pumped him about Tommie Sue. She never mentioned any family in her sessions with him. In fact, he told us she was quite resistant to delving into anything below the surface. Also, she seemed angry most of the time but denied feeling that way."

"And Phillip didn't know she and Hilda were friends?"

"I asked him that directly, if there was any indication from either Hilda or Tommie Sue, and he said not."

"I wouldn't put it past them, Trish. They both had secret lives. Hilda was into all sorts of kinky sex, and Tommie Sue was in need of a girlfriend."

"That's interesting speculation, Helen, but we won't know unless the police talk to Tommie Sue. The gal in Nevada said Phillip appeared to be a regular guy. No off-color remarks to anyone, according to her sources. Beverly also said he frequented Barnes & Noble quite a bit. He'd sit there and read, but never imposed himself on anyone."

SIXTY-THREE

"Hi, Dr. Trish. Did I hear you're getting married?"

"Sure thing, Clyde. What's the word on the street?"

"Quiet as the church house on Saturday night. Still no progress on the murder case you were interested in. Hilda's. They still be wantin' to talk to Tommie Sue Brantley, but she done evaporated. Didn't ya'll say she was seein' somebody for therapy at ya'll's clinic?"

"Yes, but she had stopped coming last spring. The funny thing is, the therapist she saw also had a relationship with Hilda. He told me Hilda was his soul mate, and as a result, they were giving up the sex-club lifestyle.

"He seems devastated by her death. I ran into him in Vegas, and he appears a changed man. For all that he was into he did pay his taxes, so the Feds aren't after him."

"Did he have any ideas about finding Tommie Sue?"

"Said that his guess was by now she's living as a 'he.'"

"Clyde, remember that murder case a few years back involving a medical center doc, the Ph.D. post doc fellow stabbed to death?"

"Sure do. We never had enough to indict Ramirez or anyone else. Between you and me, there was some sloppy police work on that one."

"Do you think he did it, Clyde?"

"Probably, but we'll never prove it. He left town anyway. Good riddance, I say."

"I saw him when we were in Key West. I looked in the

phone book and, sure enough, he's listed under Internal Medicine.

"What's always puzzled me about Hilda's body is, how did it get in the bathtub? And another thing, there were a lot of keys to the building and to the alarm system. Everybody from landscape people up to the manager had access to a key at one time or other. Anyone could have made an extra key and returned the assigned key long before the need arose for it."

"I think the killer wanted the body found far from where the initial blow to the head occurred. Maybe he even thought she was dead from the skull bashing. So why rip out her throat?"

"We think that was pure anger and rage, a desire to mutilate and further mar her body. If that hadn't been done, she would have died from the head trauma. No, this killer wants the world to know his rage."

"Clyde, you keep saying 'he.'"

"I suppose it could have been a woman. A very strong woman. Even though the victim wasn't that big, it would take a strong person to carry her to the tub. And that cut across her throat required not only a sharp instrument but strength as well."

"Maybe two people were involved."

"That's a possibility Dr. Trish. It certainly would've made transferring her body easier."

"Do you think Tommie Sue was the killer?"

"Anyone who was an associate of Hilda is under suspicion, and she's the only one we know about who hasn't been questioned. There are probably a lot of customers, if you want to call them that, who might like to see her dead. Also, the criminal element in New Orleans was most likely none too happy to have that cash cow dry up."

"If what Phillip says is true, they both had a change of heart. And plenty of money to boot. Dr. Phillip Atwater is living off his investments. So, what now, Clyde?"

"The reality of police work is that we have more than enough unsolved murders, especially ones like this. When they occur without premeditation, we often get a conviction, but this one is the kind that sits open, sometimes for years."

SIXTY-FOUR

The wedding itself, went off without incident. However, at the reception, Constance, a prim friend of Trish's mother, noticed the rector's fly was unzipped and quietly informed him.

Later, she said, "It would have ruined every picture he was in, and I wanted Trish to have a perfect photo album of the happy occasion."

If only she would have left it to informing the poor man. He quickly sought to correct the situation, and in his haste, zipped part of his shirt into it. Constance tried to be helpful, which only made matters worse.

Those close by thought too much champagne was flowing, and the rector's red face didn't help the situation. As she bent over, fumbling at the zipper in a futile effort to free the shirttail, her bright Fuchsia and gold dress only brought more attention to the scene. As a result, there were a few interesting photos from the cameras that had been placed on each table.

The wedding cake was a delight, with white chocolate ribbons and roses.

"I don't care if chocolate is supposed to be for the groom's cake, I want chocolate."

So, it was. And, as predicted, the onion sandwiches were a big hit. Surprisingly, the church organist played a great jazz piano background for the reception. 'A very nice To-Do' was the main remark as the last guests followed the happy couple to their car, gaily blowing bubbles.

It was a quick drive to New Orleans, a not-long-enough night, and a short flight to the Islands.

❁

SIXTY-FIVE

It was the season of black lace in northernmost Mississippi. Another two or three days, and spring would bring a greening to all. The blue sky, a stark background for the blackened, twisted oak limbs that spread across the scene, gave a somber note to an otherwise glorious, cold spring day. The old cemetery was green and gold with patches of daffodils. The small group of twenty or so stood graveside, wrapped in scarves and gloves, screening their faces from the brisk wind as they listened to the service.

Trish bit her lips as tears welled up. "He was such a sweet old man, Steven. I wish you had known him. I know I'm not family, but I felt the need to drive up here."

The judge had died in his sleep just two weeks after Mazie, his beloved wife of some 51 years.

After the service as Steven helped Trish into the car, she leaned over and puked her lunch onto the bright green grass.

"Are you all right?"

"I feel okay. Everything is okay, Steven. It's just my first bout of morning, or rather afternoon sickness."

"We're pregnant?" asked Steven, breathless. "It must have happened on our honeymoon."

"Can I get you anything for the ride home?"

"No, I'll be fine. I'm better now. We can think of names on the drive."

The next few weeks felt like endless months as Trish was miserable with morning sickness. "You never told me," she moaned to Barbara.

"I've always heard bad morning sickness, good baby, Trish."

"That's not much consolation now."

"No joke. How are things going?"

"Actually, great. Except this. Steven is wonderful and my OB says everything is fine. We're fairly certain it's a boy and only one, thank God. We'll know for sure on the next ultrasound."

Sheila popped her head through the doorway of Trish's new office, "Thought you'd like to see this letter. It's from lawyers so it might be important. I hate to say it, Dr. Trish, but you're letting mail pile up in your box these days."

"Hand it here. I have other things on my mind these days," Trish snapped.

Barbara made a move to leave.

"No, stay. This won't take but a minute. Well, it might."

Trish opened the thick envelope. She unfolded the heavy stock weight paper with an impressive letterhead and read aloud, "'The enclosed letter addressed to you was found among the papers of the late Judge Neville. Since the family had no interest in it, and it appears of a personal nature, we have passed it on to you. Sincerely, Travis Youngblood.'"

Clare entered the office. "What's up?"

"We're reading a letter from the grave, so to speak, from Judge Neville. Welcome. Now, if we only had Helen, we could have the complete team."

"Team?" asked Barb.

"That's how I think of us, a team, especially with our morbid curiosity in sleuthing, before Steven and the baby came on the scene, and I dropped out."

"Oh, yes, Hilda's murder. We haven't been much help. I hear they still haven't arrested anyone," said Barb. "Read us the letter."

"'Dearest Trish. I hope this letter finds you well. I'm afraid it will not find me in the same state. To be quite honest, I have not been feeling well of late. Nothing exactly to put my finger on; however, I am not asking for any medical opinion from you, as I have an appointment with my physician next week. Having ample time these days to merely sit and allow thoughts to drift through my mind, I have spent considerable hours on the matter of the event I perceived from my hotel window last summer and the finding of the business card, which you so kindly identified for me. The stain and its unusual odor has also been a matter of curiosity for me, especially since it was familiar in a subtle way. There was, I believe, a combination of bergamot, clary sage, cardamom, and a hint of patchouli.'"

Barb interrupted, "The old guy used his nose like we use the *mass spect* today."

"'In my view, a rather strange combination. As we discussed, I think it was an oily preparation, possibly a hair pomander. Now, why it was on the wall of a building is another mystery. I propose that an altercation of sorts occurred, and the party wearing this unusual substance was pushed, or shoved, against the wall, resulting in the smudge. A light to moderate shove would not result in the head hitting the wall with sufficient force to leave a mark such as I observed.'"

"The old guy had a funny way with words, didn't he?" said Clare.

"He was from the 'the old school,' as he used to say," replied Trish, "but don't sell him short, he had a keen mind. Let me continue."

"'I suspect the crumpled business card was dropped by the assailant, if that is the proper term, and probably in anger, as the card was quite wrinkled, but fresh in appearance, not weathered. I am afraid this is all I have to offer. I thought you might be interested, as you told me the unfortunate woman who was murdered last summer had an association with the Notti's establishment.

"'I have a premonition I shall be taking a journey soon

across the river Styx, never to return. Sincerely yours, Wallace Neville.'"

"What's he talking about, a journey across the river? I've never heard of the Styx?" said Barb.

"It's from Greek mythology, the underworld. He's talking about his death. What's the date on the letter, Trish?" said Clare. "One week before his death," sighed Trish, as she refolded letter. "What do you gals think of that?"

"What do you mean?" asked Barbara.

"The old guy was an astute observer. I think we three had better get Helen in on this. We need to do a little brainstorming, thinking outside the box, as to whether this incident had any connection to Hilda's death. It occurred only a couple of days before her body was found in the bathtub. If we go talk to the police now, they'll write us off as a bunch of kooky females."

"How about this Saturday? We can have some of Helen's famous chicken salad sandwiches for lunch and stir our collective brain pot and see what bubbles up." said Trish.

"Sure thing," said Barb.

"Steven plans to sail, poor baby; he hasn't gone out as much as usual lately. We'll have the house to ourselves. See ya'll Saturday noon, sharp," said Trish, "and in the meantime, allow a new gestalt to form with the data we have."

Alone in her office, Trish allowed her mind to drift back to the unsolved murder. Maybe I should let my preconscious right brain tackle this. I'm sure not getting anywhere otherwise. And that scent that Judge Neville identified. What, if anything, did it have to do with the entire situation?

Getting up quietly, she turned off the overhead fluorescent light, leaving only the afternoon light drifting through the window blind, making slippery shadows across the room. Trish closed her eyes. Tilting back in the desk chair, she allowed herself to enter a slight dissociative state she preferred to call a light trance, knowing full well some of her best ideas came to her when she took the time to do this. Suddenly she sat up, alert.

❀

Phillip. Dr. A. That junk he used to put on his hair. It had a funny scent. Could it be the same? But what could that have to do with the smudge the old judge smelled? Maybe other men wore it.

Trish didn't think so.

Maybe it's popular with a group I never come in contact with or see. I'll have to give Dr. Atwater a call and ask him.

❀

SIXTY-SIX

That evening, from home, Trish dialed the Vegas number.

"Phil, Trish McLeod here. I hope I'm not interrupting you or anything."

"No, I was just reading. I do a lot of that, and meditation. Used to like porn videos. Now I'm thinking I'll sell them. There's a market for them here in Vegas. I find that after I check the news once a day, other TV holds no interest for me these days."

"I realize this may sound stupid, Phil, but remember the preparation you used on your hair?"

"That greasy, smelly gunk?"

"I'm surprised you label it the way most of us around here did. What was it? And what, more specifically, was the scent in it?"

"It was a personally formulated cologne at first, then I had it incorporated into a standard hair dressing. Some of the ingredients were purported to have an aphrodisiac effect. I never found that to be particularly true, however. I can get the address in New York where it was made, if you want. They make all kinds of personal fragrances."

"Do you know of anyone else who used that particular fragrance?"

"We kept a small supply at the club for sale. I really didn't keep up with sales. That was more Hilda's job. I had extra because it was cheaper to have it made up in a larger quantity. Why are you asking? You didn't like it, did you?"

"No, to be honest, I found it a little sickening. Do you remember any of the herbs that went into it?"

"There was bergamot, clary sage, and a touch of smoky labdamerm and elemi, I remember those. There were several more ingredients. If you didn't like it, why are you asking me about it? I threw out all that I had. It reminded me of the old days. I stopped using it about the time Hilda was killed. It just didn't fit me anymore."

"Phillip, I know you didn't kill Hilda because you were at your sister's, but I needed to know what was in that stuff. Thanks."

❧

SIXTY-SEVEN

"Let's eat on the patio today. It's nice out," said Trish, as Helen entered the kitchen on Saturday carrying a couple of large grocery bags.

"Sounds good to me. I brought some homemade potato chips to go with the chicken salad sandwiches, fruit salad with mini marshmallows, my to-die-for poppy seed dressing, a bottle of Peach Ice Tea concentrate, and a few fresh chocolate chip cookies."

"Great, Helen! You're quite the gourmet cook these days. That ought to feed our brains. Set the food out on the patio while I grab a pitcher and mix the tea."

Clare and Barbara arrived just as Helen was filling the tall glasses with iced tea.

"To us!" toasted Barb.

"We ought to have a name," said Helen, "like a club."

"Let us know when you come up with one. So, down to business," said Trish. "Anything new arise from our collective minds?"

Clare said, "I'll start. I keep coming back to how Hilda was carried or dragged into that clinic. That took access and some strength. Barbara, what do you think?"

"I keep going back to the oily smudge and the card the old judge found from the sex club. I wonder if somehow it's connected, but no plausible connection comes to mind."

Helen piped up, "And what about Tommie Sue, her friend who has now disappeared? Remember, Hilda and Tommie Sue were both interested in gardening and were members of the Green Garden Gang. Both were familiar, to some extent, with the clinic. We know they did some landscape work there last spring."

"I guess you all know that Dr. Phillip Atwater saw Tommie Sue as a patient at the university outpatient psych clinic," Trish interjected.

"What for, Trish?"

"She was going for some minor depression and the one-year required counseling prior to sex surgery. Her chart didn't show that she was transsexual—believed she was a man trapped in a woman's body, not a lesbian."

"Really, now, and she was friends with Hilda? Maybe they were more than gardening buddies."

"That's possible. It appears Hilda was game for any and everything imaginable in the sex arena."

"It's standard practice to have transsexuals see a therapist," said Clare. "She was taking male hormones and already had undergone surgery to remove her ovaries. He also had her on antidepressants, and the last progress note at the clinic said "depression resolving, no longer having suicidal thoughts or feelings of hopelessness.'"

"I'd bet she found a significant other, probably female."

"Then she just stopped coming? How long before Hilda's death was that?" asked Barb.

"At least two to three months."

Clare asked, "Does anyone think Hilda knew Tommie Sue was seeing her 'main man,' Phillip Atwater?"

Trish replied, "Probably not. Although Phillip had his problems with boundaries and was lax in many ways, I doubt he would tell Hilda the name of any patient he was seeing. Anyway, Tommie Sue had stopped seeing him for therapy by then, and according to Phillip, the realization of the true nature of his relationship with Hilda didn't develop until nearly June."

"Maybe Tommie Sue mentioned her therapist's name to Hilda," said Helen, "especially if they were close."

"Now that's more likely and plausible."

Clare said, "We need to ask Phillip point-blank if he was anywhere near that corner where the judge found the smudge."

"Okay," said Trish. "I'll call him now and ask." Flipping open her pocket address book, she quickly punched in the numbers.

"Hello, Phillip. This is Trish McLeod again. I hate to bother you, but were you anywhere near a hotel in downtown Gulfport, a few days to a week before Hilda was killed? No? What about staff from the club or someone who might have one of your business cards from Notti's?" Trish was silent for a few minutes. "That's all you remember? Thanks a lot Phillip."

"What did he say?" asked Clare.

"He said he wasn't in the area, but it was one of the locations where money transfers were made."

"Money transfers? What are you talking about?" said Helen.

"They paid a fee, or kickback, I don't know what to call it. Anyway, the mob, for lack of a better name, took a cut of the profits from the club and usually sent a representative to pick it up. Not every week and not always at the same place. They varied the pick up point."

"So, who from the club took the funds?" said Barbara.

"He said Hilda was in charge of that, but she wasn't always the one who did the actual delivery. She might ask someone else who worked for the club to do it, not telling them what was in the package. It was the last part of June when Phillip informed the people in New Orleans he was thinking of closing the club soon. He wasn't sure when the last delivery occurred."

"But didn't you say what the judge saw happened in July?"

"Yep. That's what he said."

"So, what he saw wasn't a drop?"

"Doesn't look like that's what he had a glimpse of."

"So, we have two people on that corner sometime in early July who had an encounter. We think one of them wore the same hair dressing Phillip did, and somehow it was smeared on the wall, enough of it that a few minutes later the judge could smell it."

"Okay, girls," said Trish, "let's speculate. We can say anything we want. We're not talking to the police or anything."

"Maybe he was a person from New Orleans, 'cause we don't think anybody else around here used that stuff on their hair."

"So, Mr. Greasy, for want of a better name, might have been a customer or client of the club, or possibly, he was an employee, so to speak, of the mob."

"Or an employee of the club," chimed in Clare, "and he's talking to another person, unknown to us."

"Hell! They're both unknown," said Barbara.

"Point taken," said Trish, "they are both unknown to us. However, they apparently had words, and one of them, Mr. Greasy, was slammed up against the wall hard enough to leave an oily sample of his hair product. What could Mr. Greasy have said that made other party so angry that he shoved him against the wall?"

"That the sex club was closing or had closed?" said Helen. "There was the crumpled card. Maybe the other person was a client or wanted to be a client and was pissed off at not having his jollies?"

"Or," Clare spoke up, "it was someone hitting Mr. Greasy up for money. Or what if Mr. Greasy was a mob representative and this other person threatened to rat on the club, telling the cops or the media?"

"So, two people had an argument, and a curious old man just happened to see it. What could that have to do with Hilda's death?" continued Trish.

"Probably nothing. Phillip said he wasn't in that area, and how many people used that hair preparation? Very few. Whoever used it most likely bought it at the club, the only source for it," said Barb.

Clare added, "I think this is a dead end. The most likely person who did the shoving was pissed off that the club was closing and shoved Mr. Greasy. Maybe he had paid in advance for some special service, and now it wasn't going to happen."

"Well, this has been fun, girls," said Helen. "I give us all an 'F' for detective-sleuth work. We still have no idea who killed Hilda."

"Wait. Let's do another fantasy trip," suggested Clare. "Pretend I'm the one who killed Hilda. Let's profile the killer like they talk about on TV."

"Okay," said Trish. "You're crafty Clare who kills with care. How did you do it?"

Clare launched into her scenario. "I'm really angry, in a rage, at Hilda. I'm a customer of the club, and she set up all kinds of special entertainment for me that I can't get elsewhere. I like sadomasochistic tricks, chains and whips sometimes. Hilda has informed me the club is closing. I hit her with something big on the back of her head as she's walking away from me."

"A shovel," piped in Helen.

"No, if that was the case it didn't happen on the corner. And it probably wasn't Hilda on the corner anyway," said Barb. "Maybe later. Somewhere else."

"Okay, that's a possibility. So I really whack her, at some unknown location, she falls, and I think she's dead. So now I'm faced with a body. What to do with it? I remember the mental health clinic, and decide that if I stash the body there, no one will know where it happened."

"How'd you get in?" said Helen.

Clare said, "Pretend it was a shovel, and this person is a gardener who has worked with the Green Garden Gang at the clinic. I have a key, and because the Gang did some work on a Saturday, I needed and used the key and never returned it."

"Okay, so far," said Helen, "but how did you know there was a bathtub in the clinic?"

"If I were made a member of the Garden Gang, a woman member could have used that toilet and shared the info, like, 'You all would never believe what's in that toilet.' sort of thing."

"But, Clare, that restroom is on the second floor. Wouldn't someone using the john on a weekend just go to the closest one?" asked Barbara.

"Probably, but what if I was nosey? What if I looked around, checked to see what was unlocked?"

"Well enough," said Trish. "A female from the Garden Gang might have said to the group, 'Guess what? There's a bathtub in the women's toilet on the second floor,' and the killer remembered this. But I wonder why the killer chose the clinic? Because of the name? Did he make some weird connection that the appropriate place for Hilda had something to do with mental health?"

"Hers or his?" said Helen.

"Either," said Trish. "Since we are pretending, let's go to the extreme. One thing we haven't considered. If he thought she was dead, why slit her throat?"

"Yes, we don't know why that was done," said Barb. "Whoever did that was in a rage," said Trish, "and strong."

"It must have been premeditated because the killer brought the knife with him to the clinic," said Clare. "Maybe he wanted to mutilate her so she would be of no sexual interest. She was an attractive gal, after all."

"Yes," said Trish, "but that slash was vicious. There was a lot more behind it than making her unattractive. And the killer was careful at the clinic, remember? No prints."

"Latex gloves?" asked Helen.

"They're easily available. Even Wal-Mart has them. So, what's our choice now? One person, the killer? All in favor, raise your hand."

"Trish, he had to be strong," said Helen.

"A strong man. Do we have anything to tell the police?"

"I don't see what," said Clare. "We're just supposing. I suggest we talk to the members of the Green Garden Gang who were on the team that worked at the clinic. Maybe one of them would remember who was in charge of the key to the clinic."

"I think we should approach it from two directions. Helen, you're a member of the Garden Club. Possibly some of the members of the Green Garden Gang are also members of your garden club. And Clare, you're now a Green Garden Gang member."

Trish continued, "I don't see anything more we can do. We sure don't have anything to tell the police. Clyde says that when a case goes this long, it's frequently impossible to solve. How soon do you think you can do what we've asked, Helen?"

"We're having a meeting Monday, so I'll go for sure. Those gals in the Garden Club just aren't my type anymore, too social and snobby for me. I don't know what I ever saw in them anyway."

Barb said, "Let's not wait another week to meet. Helen, could you call us after the meeting and let's meet on Tuesday? This is beginning to occupy too much of my attention. I need to get it resolved, or say it's over and move on."

"Sure, and ya'll come to my house. Reggie will be at his meeting Tuesday night anyway. "Say 7:00?"

❁

SIXTY-EIGHT

Helen's house, lovely as usual and clearly a step above mine, Trish thought as she entered the spacious foyer with its fine oriental rug and antique English chest-on-chest. *At least it looks antique to me.* She eyed the massive silk flower arrangement centered on the fully extended Mahogany dining table. That alone cost a bundle, at least $400.

Trish passed through to the large, comfortable den family room with overstuffed sofas and chairs. The only exception to the décor was an old tweedy brown La-Z-Boy recliner situated a comfortable distance from the oversized entertainment center.

"Reggie just wouldn't budge on that," said Helen, when she noticed the direction of Trish's gaze.

Clare and Barbara had already claimed their spots.

"Anything to drink?" asked Helen, always the gracious hostess.

"No thanks," was the group's reply.

Trish was first to speak. "What did you find out, Helen?"

"I don't know if any of this will be helpful, but I verified that Hilda worked with the Green Garden Gang from time to time, but not in the group that worked at the clinic."

"Did you speak to anyone who did?" asked Barbara.

"Margaret, who's the least snobby member of the club, chatted with me. She worked at the clinic last spring. In fact, she said they were there three Saturdays."

"Did they have a key?"

"She said they had two keys, one for the door and one for the alarm. No one in particular kept them."

"Did she ever go inside to get a drink or use the toilet?" asked Trish.

"Yes, on several occasions, but she only went to the first floor and said she didn't know there was a bathtub anywhere."

"Did she remember the names of any of the other workers?"

"She didn't know all of them. She said it was a large group. A lot bigger than other groups she's worked with, at least twelve. They planted a lot of annuals, some trees, and did some pruning."

"So, what names did she give you?" said Clare.

"The one that surprised me was Tommie Sue Brantley. Margaret said that she'd been on several teams with her and tried to be friendly, but Tommie Sue gave her the cold shoulder. In fact, Margaret said she was always moody. There were quite a few men, more than usual, on the team, and she remembered one of the regulars introduced his friend who was visiting from Florida, John something, and the thought passed through Margaret's mind that they were lovers."

"I don't think Margaret would say something like that. There must have been something to make her come up with it."

"Did you pump her?" said Trish.

"A little. She said it was just a thought, nothing specific. When they took a lunch break, Tommie Sue sat with the male couple, and they were a group unto themselves, not chatty with the rest. Margaret thought that strange, as those gardening expeditions usually are as much social as civic service. In fact, she commented that during the past four or five years she has volunteered, there have been some types that volunteered a time or two, received their green tee shirt, and were never seen again. They needed to have some community service on their resume, that sort of thing."

"Is that what she thought of the guy and his friend from Florida?"

"Yes, that's what she thought. She only saw the one guy three or four times and the friend from Florida that once at the clinic project."

"I wonder if they knew Hilda?" said Trish.

Helen replied, "Margaret said Hilda wasn't on any of the jobs at the clinic project."

"What did these guys look like?" asked Clare.

"Well, Margaret thought they were unremarkable and clean-cut. The one from Florida although older, was tanned and muscular like maybe he did weight training. She said he and Tommie Sue handled the shovels. They planted several Crepe Myrtles."

"That doesn't mean Hilda didn't know them. Remember how she came after my Reggie that spring?"

"What?" exclaimed Clare.

"Oh, nothing. Reggie had a couple of business lunches with Hilda and told me she was very seductive," replied Helen.

Some things are better left unsaid, thought Trish.

Out loud she said, "Anyone on that work team could now have a key to the clinic. From what I've discovered, clinic staff are not careful with their keys. Maybe they are now, after a corpse was found in the building. As long as nothing was missing, they just let things slide. I've seen it before. A disaster or tragedy has to occur to result in tightening or enforcing procedures or protocols already in place. Helen, did the team store any of their equipment or supplies in the clinic?"

"I asked and Margaret said the fertilizer and topsoil purchased by the clinic, and a few tools, were stored in the basement crawl space under the inside stairs near a side entrance. Most of the garden team had their own tools, like trowels, rakes, and some had sharpshooter shovels."

"Gal gang, are we any farther along on our sleuthing?" asked Trish.

"I'm afraid not," said Barbara.

"One more thing, and I'll give this up and get on with my life," said Trish. "I'll ask Clyde if the police looked at that crawlspace under the clinic. Or, I might just look myself the next time I'm out there."

"Trish, you're pregnant. Do you think you should?" said Helen.

"I'm not that far along. Want to look with me?"

"Sure," said Helen, "tell me when."

"I'm scheduled to go out tomorrow morning. Drop by my office, and we'll go on my coffee break."

❀

SIXTY-NINE

Clyde was ensconced in his darkened office in front of a miniscule TV, watching *Good Morning America*, when Trish passed by. She backtracked, stuck her head inside and said, "Clyde, did the detectives check out the crawl space under the stairs near the side door of the clinic when investigating Hilda's murder?"

"I don't remember anyone saying anything about a crawl space. Where is it again?"

"I'll show you. I'll come back at coffee break time," said Trish.

For once, all three scheduled patients kept their appointments. Trish rushed to see them and dictated a brief evaluation on each. As she turned to go downstairs to Clyde's office, Helen stepped off the elevator.

"Perfect timing, Helen. Let's take the stairs. Clyde wants to go also."

"So, where's this crawl space, Dr. Trish?" Clyde questioned, as they arrived at the back side door.

"Here, under the stairs."

The door was adjacent to the second floor stairs and set back from the hall.

"Bless my soul, I never noticed it before."

"They store janitorial supplies down there."

"Okay, let's look. Glory be, it's open! I guess Brian didn't lock it the last time he was here," said Clyde.

"Why am I not surprised?" said Trish. Crouching down, so as not to hit her head, Trish led the way down the steps to the dirt-floored space, cluttered with cans of what looked to be floor wax, paints of different colors, old brooms, bags of fertilizer, an artificial Christmas tree, collapsing cardboard boxes, and a stack of newspapers.

"Nothing here, Trish."

"Let's look under the steps, Helen. Clyde, shine your flashlight under here."

"Just a bunch of garden tools, Dr. Trish."

"Look, a shovel. I think you'd better call your favorite detective to come check this out."

"Don't touch anything, Dr. Trish."

"I'm not that stupid. I'm just looking."

"I'll go call him," said Clyde, as he started back up the steps.

"We'll be along in a minute," said Trish, sweeping the flashlight over the tools. "Helen, look. There's a dark rusty patch on that shovel. It doesn't look like dirt."

"Maybe it's what Hilda was hit on the back of the head with. Didn't you tell me that?" Helen responded.

"Yes, I did. I guess we'd better wait in my office for a while. The detective may want to talk to us. I'll ask Clyde."

As Helen sat on the blue sofa in Trish's office, Trish called Clyde.

"Do we have to hang around? Good, you have my number. We saw a dark stain—I didn't touch anything, I swear, just looked. It was on a shovel. Will you let me know if it turns out to be Hilda's blood? Thanks."

Turning to Helen, Trish said, "We're free to leave. The detective won't need to talk to us, but he'll probably grill Clyde as to why he happened to look in the crawl space.

"Call me tonight. We need to talk. Looks as if we'll need another meeting of our gang. Four heads are better than one. Tomorrow, my house this time," said Trish as they exited the clinic to their cars.

"Trish, I don't want to talk to any detective."

"Not to worry. Clyde will come up with some plausible reason as to why he happened to look down there. Call around seven."

❋

SEVENTY

"Group's in session," said Clare.

"Ha, ha," replied Trish.

"Just commenting. We're a group now, and process happens whether it's a therapy group or not," retorted Clare.

"Well, we aren't a therapy group, although we may be therapeutic," said Barb.

"Everyone cool? Anyone need something to drink? I don't want to miss anything," said Trish.

Each woman had selected the same spot as the previous meeting at Trish's house.

"We're creatures of habit, are we not?" said Clare as Helen made the observation.

"So, where are we with this, Trish?" said Barb.

"Did any of you see the evening news? They found a shovel with what appeared to be bloodstains at the clinic."

"No way!" said Barb. "Do you think it was 'the' shovel?"

"I do," said Trish. "Clyde called just before ya'll arrived to report that he told the detective he hadn't thought to look behind that door because he didn't know it was there. A large stack of empty ceiling tile boxes had completely hidden the door at the time of the murder and for a number of months after."

"So much for efficiency. Those boxes were a fire code violation too."

"Anyway, Clyde didn't get grilled too badly."

"Did the shovel belong to the clinic?"

"Brian, the maintenance man, didn't think so. He never

looked under those stairs in the five years he worked there. He was somewhat abashed to admit he has a morbid fear of spiders."

"I suggest that the killer placed the shovel there after bashing poor Hilda," said Helen.

"I'll bet anything there aren't any fingerprints on it."

"I'd be surprised if there were," said Helen.

"So," said Barbara, "do we still think Hilda was hit and carried into the clinic, or was she inside the clinic when she was whacked?"

"Why would she be inside a mental health clinic at midnight?" asked Helen.

"Because she was unconscious and was carried?" said Trish.

"Time to think outside the box again," said Clare. "Shoot. Anyone? Don't censor anything that comes to your feeble minds."

"We should agree beforehand that none of us will criticize or think negative thoughts about anything that comes out," said Helen. "I don't know you all as well as you know each other, and I'm worried you'll think I'm a weirdo if I come up with something strange."

"Not to worry, Helen," said Clare, "even if you suggest that aliens helped."

Helen continued. "Then let's suppose the killer was a customer of Hilda's, and he was the one who slammed Mr. Greasy Hair against the wall when he heard his favorite club and source of entertainment was closing."

"But is that any reason to kill her?" said Trish.

"Not if it was only that," said Clare. "Maybe there was a little more to it than the club closing."

"Like what?" asked Barb.

Helen speculated. "What if he was a control freak and getting lots of special sexual adventures from Hilda? If that was the only way he could 'get it up,' he would be furious. And if he couldn't have her, no one else would either."

"Why the mental health clinic?"

"Maybe he arranged for a sexual encounter there. Talked her into one farewell fling, as it were," said Barb.

"Or," said Helen, "it happened somewhere else, and he carried her body to the clinic."

"With this line of thought, we're saying it was one of those guys on the Green Garden Gang team?" said Clare.

"Maybe yes, maybe no. Those keys could have been passed to almost anyone," said Barb.

"I'm confused," said Trish. "Remember that Hilda, according to Phillip, had a change of heart. They were soul mates. She was opting out of the sex business."

"Or so he thought," quipped Clare.

"Let's sum up where we are," continued Trish. "Hilda had a secret life, and someone was really pissed off enough to kill her because she was starting a new life without him anywhere in it. Phillip was convinced she was going to marry him and leave the sex business. Hilda did lots of quirky, kinky sex for clients, customers, or whatever she called them. Her new soul mate, Phillip, was out of town to tell his sister of their wonderful relationship and new life to come.

"Realize, girls, I'm being a little dramatic here, and I find myself not really believing the words. I think Phillip was a changed person, but not Hilda."

"Or," said Clare, "she had changed but agreed to one last encounter with the killer. Maybe something she had contracted for, or been paid money to arrange, something special, and the customer threatened to expose her if she didn't follow through. After all, she planned to marry a university professor, a blackmail for one farewell act."

Helen said, "I think the police should question everyone on the Green Garden Gang who worked at the clinic."

"Clyde can suggest it, but I'd bet, after finding the shovel, they're already onto that trail," said Trish.

"I vote for the stranger from Florida," said Helen. "Now, where did you come up with that?" said Barbara.

"Let's say he came up for special things that Hilda arranged, maybe with his friend who lives here. He was strong, he had access to the keys."

"Helen, that's really a shot in the dark," said Trish.

"I don't think so," returned Helen. "It would fit in with what Clare suggested, something was arranged at another location. Hilda told him, or them, that this was the last time. Maybe the killer went into a rage because what Hilda did for him or arranged for him was the only way he wasn't impotent. I don't have any idea what it could be, maybe something not ordinarily available from a prostitute."

"Helen, that doesn't sound as far out as I first thought. I'm sure the police will question all the Green Garden Gang now," said Trish.

"That," said Clare, "could also explain the need for slashing her throat. If we want to wax analytical, the killer might have some childhood memory or event associated with a bathtub, and we've already agreed there was some planning to the murder. The initial blow to the head could have been done in a loss of control rage—grabbing a shovel—but, after that, the killer was deliberate, whether the shovel blow occurred at the clinic or at another location."

"I vote for another location," said Helen.

"Helen, honey, we don't need to vote," said Clare.

Helen continued, "What I mean is, if the shovel blow occurred there, how'd he have the shovel at hand? A shovel wouldn't just have been leaning against a wall in a clinic at midnight for him to use. He had to have hit her at another location."

They all agreed with Helen on that point.

"So, if the killer is one of the men who worked on the team and overheard a woman member say there was a bathtub on the second floor, it clicked with something from his childhood. So, he went looking for the tub after he carried Hilda into the building," said Barb. "The police most likely will ask all those gardeners about the tub and if it was mentioned to the group."

"Boy, is that a stretch. No wonder we aren't police detectives," said Clare.

Trish replied, "Well, this closes the mystery as far as I'm concerned. Too bad the police haven't been able to talk to Tommie Sue Brantley. She was the one, according to Margaret, who chatted with those guys."

"I'm still wondering," said Clare, "about the mystery man from Florida. How did he happen to have a shovel handy?"

Helen replied, "Maybe he didn't, but the local guy did. Some people really into gardening have their own tools they carry to every site. It's like a chef's 'personal knives.'"

"He could have taken the knife and gloves from the place where he hit her, so maybe it was an apartment or condo, someplace with a kitchen."

"Maybe it was Hilda's townhouse," said Helen.

"We'll never know unless there's a confession," said Trish. "I wonder if Hilda kept personal gardening tools at her place? I'll keep ya'll posted as to anything I hear from Clyde regarding the Green Garden Gang."

Clare pointed out, "We seem to have formed a little friends' group because of our morbid curiosity. Too bad it's over."

Helen replied, "We're still friends. I like getting together. Maybe we can do lunch once a month or so."

"Great idea!" said Clare. "Remember the baby shower on Sunday afternoon, week after next, at my place."

"Getting excited about the baby, Trish?" asked Helen.

"Yes, and I'm seriously considering a very long maternity leave, maybe six months. I have that much sick leave accumulated."

SEVENTY-ONE

Two weeks later, at the baby shower, Trish asked Helen and Barb to stay afterwards, as she had some news on their sleuthing to share.

It was another forty minutes before the last guest made her departure after 'ooing' and 'ahhing' over the lovely party.

"God! I thought they'd never leave," exclaimed Clare. "Quick, let's hear what you've heard, Trish! Have they a suspect, any arrest imminent?"

"Clyde told me they questioned all those folks who worked on the garden team at the clinic."

"And?" interrupted Barb.

"Looks like another dead end," finished Trish.

"What?" exclaimed Helen, "What about all the things we figured out at our meeting?"

"Some of them might be true," said Trish, "but not the part about the guys who worked on the team at the clinic last spring."

"Oh, what a disappointment," said Helen. "I was so sure we had figured it out."

"I thought so, too," said Trish, "but Clyde said all of them had alibis, except they haven't been able to locate Tommie Sue Brantley."

Clare said, "I think she's no longer Tommie Sue, but Tom somebody, with a fake ID."

"She's still Tommie Sue from a biological standpoint. No way to get a y-chromosome, no matter how much she believed she was a man trapped in a woman's body," said Barbara.

"This really looks like the end of our detective work. Now, we'll just have to be a lunch bunch."

"I always try to look for something positive," said Clare. "Sure, Hilda's death was tragic, and her life was tragic until she and Phillip met. At least, we four have become friends. That's how I feel."

"Me, too," chimed in the other three.

"So, let's take what good has come out of this and move on," Clare finished.

❁

"It's a lot hotter than it was last summer," said Trish, as she and Clare sat in the shade behind Clare's house a few weeks later.

"Oh, it's about the same. You're just pregnant," teased Clare.

"Let's not go there. I've had more than I need of 'when I was pregnant' stories. I think we'll get a break in a couple of hours from the look of those clouds. I hope Steven is on his way back to shore."

"I wouldn't worry over a little thunder shower. As much experience as he has, it will be a piece of cake," said Clare.

"Clare, my mind keeps wandering back to ol' Phillip Atwater. Do you think he really changed?"

"I suppose anything is possible, but we both know a person with a Narcissistic Personality Disorder is so well defended that not many of them really ever change. He sure gave us a line in Vegas, and he had changed in appearance before he saw us," said Clare.

Trish continued, "Let's back off and not talk about Phillip specifically, but just Narcissistic Personalities."

"Okay."

"I think there has to be a significant external environmental pressure, or change if you will, before one would even consider thinking or acting any differently," said Trish.

"The ones I remember," replied Clare, "who effected a change, frequently had legal problems, financial problems, or serious threats, and the change was of location, not personality. Those probably weren't in a therapeutic relationship either. I think therapy isn't effective unless the therapist is top of the line experienced."

"Could Phillip have experienced any of those things? He told us it was Hilda's death that motivated him."

"That could be true, but it is possible there were other motives," said Clare.

"He said money was no problem," Trish countered. "He didn't need to work."

"So," said Clare, "what else? Someone threatened him, and he didn't tell us? If he had been threatened, why not tell the police?"

"Maybe he had some secrets he didn't want revealed."

"What kind? He closed the sex club."

"Could Hilda's killer be after him?"

"I keep coming back to the fact that he's in therapy with one of our finest. Also, he's keeping a very low profile. We just happened to see him because he needed some continuing medical education hours to keep his medical license."

"We could be biased regarding psychotherapy, thinking it more effective and life-changing than it really is, even in the hands of an expert. We know there has to be some emotional distress for real change. And most people who suffer from a personality disorder, like Phillip, are, as we used to say, ego-syntonic, and therefore, not motivated to stay in therapy. However, he says he was in great distress over Hilda's death. He meets his soul mate and loses her before they can really share a life. He could talk rings around a traditional analytic type for years and have no real change internally."

"But remember, Harry Brown isn't that kind of therapist. He does a lot of Gestalt therapy and, as I remember from a workshop years ago, some body work. That was something to see, Clare. This patient was so defended, and when Harry put him over a bioenergic breathing stool for a couple of minutes, all kinds of shit came out from his childhood that the guy said he had not been aware of. I mean, things he swore he had no conscious memory of yet influenced how he lived his life. It would probably take something like that to delve into Phillip's psyche."

"Once again, Trish, I think we're speculating, maybe over-dramatizing a reflection of some parts of ourselves."

"Anything is possible, but this time I don't think so."

"We'll have to stop obsessing over this case after all. Did you ever hear anything from Clyde about the shovel?"

"He said, as we suspected, no fingerprints. The shovel was well-kept, oiled, and sharp, and there were a few blonde hairs with dark roots, so it was the object that crushed Hilda's skull. It took a fierce blow to crack her skull with a shovel. It wouldn't take as much strength if it had been a sledgehammer, say."

"Do they think she was hit at the clinic or hit elsewhere and brought there?"

"Clyde says most likely she was hit somewhere else and, as he put it, toted there. Remember, no prints, so gloves were probably used."

"Too bad they haven't any leads from client/customers of the sex club. One of them might have a lead. The killer may be a disgruntled customer."

"That's been checked as best they could, and according to Clyde, nothing."

❋

SEVENTY-TWO

A few weeks later Trish gave birth to a beautiful baby boy, Adam.

Now, Trish, reclining on the sofa reading a book of baby tips, thought how satisfied and happy she was. Steven was as excited as she about the baby and wanted to help. So far, he had changed several diapers and assisted earlier that morning in little Adam's first bath.

She sent him out to visit some of his buddies for a round of golf, saying, "You need a break. My mother can handle anything we need. Save your strength for later. Supper will be at 6:30."

Steven was hardly out of the drive when Helen, Clare, and Barbara arrived.

"Looks like a meeting," said Trish, after all cooed and oohed over the baby.

Adam cooperated by looking like a little angel, with dark hair like his daddy, as he slept on his back.

Just then, the doorbell chimed and Trish said, "Get that for me, will you, Helen?"

"Well, knock me over with a feather," drawled Helen. "It's our favorite policeman! Hi, Clyde."

"Hi, ladies, nice to see you. This is for the little one, Dr. Trish."

"Oh, Clyde, you shouldn't have, but thanks. How nice; a silver rattle, Thanks again. Any new crimes solved, Clyde?"

"No, but I've been promoted."

"Great!"

"Yep, I'm now officially the rank of sergeant."

"What about cold cases?" asked Barbara. "Like Hilda's?"

"No, afraid that's cold as a well diggers ass."

"Well, if anything develops, will you let us know, just as a matter of curiosity? We spent a hell of a lot of time and energy sleuthing and discussing her death."

"I really shouldn't, but ya'll contributed to my promotion by letting me find the shovel, or so the higher-ups thought. I'm sure you ladies will keep anything I say confidential like, unless or until it came out on the news."

"Of course," said Clare. "Our lips are sealed, except to each other. And I'll bet none of our husbands give a toot about our interest in Hilda's death."

"I'll keep you ladies posted."

❁

SEVENTY-THREE

Tradition for Trish was decorating the Christmas tree the first week of December. She and Steven had finished the task the night before.

"Wow, you really have a knack for decorating."

"Thanks, Helen. Come on in. The others are already here. It's really not hot chocolate weather, but we can pretend."

"I know we agreed to let this Hilda thing die, but what now, Trish?" said Clare.

"I received a Christmas card from, of all people,—"

"We know," the trio chimed in, "Phillip."

"You're right, and he wrote a little note. Said he was still in therapy and to give regards to you, Clare. Also, he doesn't think he'll ever practice medicine again."

"What do you make of that, Trish?"

"I'm not reading anything into it, but I'm sure the old Dr. Ass would never send me a Christmas card."

"Is there a return address?"

"Yes, Helen, and his e-mail. They're the same ones he gave us in Vegas."

"Was there a phone number?"

"Yes, it's the same also."

"They never did find Tommie Sue," began Barbara. "I still wonder what happened to her. Maybe we should ask Phillip again if he's ever heard from her. After all, he treated her for depression for a while until she dropped out."

"Barbara might have a point. If she were upset over Hilda's death—we don't know why she moved—and later found out where he was living, she might try to contact him for further treatment."

"How could she do that?" asked Helen.

"Oh, that's easy enough, on the Web. He has a valid license to practice medicine in several states."

"So, you're suggesting she went to Vegas to look him up?" said Clare.

"Heck! Let's call him," said Clare. "It can't hurt. Rates are cheap on the weekends. Where's that calling card, Trish?"

"Here it is," said Trish, as she shuffled a stack of cards retrieved from the coffee table drawer.

"You or me?" said Clare.

"You, Clare. He said to send you regards, so you can say I told you and you just wanted to wish him Happy Holidays."

"Won't he see through that?"

"So what? Nothing ventured, nothing gained. Look, I'll switch on the speaker, and we can all listen."

❁

SEVENTY-FOUR

"Phillip this is Clare Connor. How are you doing?"

"Great, Clare. Good to hear your voice. I sent Trish a card and told her to remember me to you."

"Yes, she told me. Thanks," Clare replied. "Are you practicing psychiatry these days?"

"No, not even medicine. I'm letting my medical license go next time it comes up for renewal."

"Phillip. The police never located Tommie Sue Brantley to question her in regard to Hilda's death. You treated her for depression. Has she tried to contact you?"

"No, she hasn't. If she kept on with the plan she spoke of the last time I saw her, she's living as a 'he,' in a relationship with a woman. I haven't thought of her in over a year, since that time we ran into each other at the American Group Meeting."

"Did you ever pick up a lot of anger or hostility when you did see her?"

"Oh, yes. She was a very angry person but at that time, would have walked over hot coals before admitting it to me or anyone else."

"Was she psychotic?"

"No, not in the usual sense, although there was one time she shared some rather bizarre sexual fantasies. As far as I know, she wasn't using street drugs, and basically she had schizoid personality traits and a few schizo-typical traits, but never enough to call her either diagnosis. She was a strange one, but look how weird I was in those days.

"I'm sorry to tell you that I took a rather haughtier-than-you attitude toward her. Remember, I was on my high horse about myself, above everyone else, and she was a dumb broad who believed she was a man trapped in a woman's body.

"That reminds me Clare. About a month ago, I saw a fellow outside the supermarket who reminded me of Tommie Sue. He gave me a hard, penetrating stare and turned, walking away before he ever came inside. I was at the checkout counter and didn't see him when I took my groceries to the car."

"Phillip, several of us 'hen' medics, and another woman friend, have become obsessed with Hilda's death. We were instrumental, although the police don't know, in locating the shovel used to hit Hilda on the head. We think, to solve the crime, the police need to talk to Tommie Sue. Hell, Phillip, we're entertaining the idea that she killed Hilda."

"Why would she?"

"We don't have a motive. Of course, there could be a client of the sex club who had it in for Hilda."

"I might bet on that, Clare."

"But the police have checked tons of VISA receipts and come up with nothing."

"Clare, most of the transactions were in cash. Most of the ones who had unusual requests, insisted on paying in cash."

"Thanks for talking to me, Phillip. Will you let Trish or me know if you think of anything or if anything unusual happens to you? We've wondered if the killer is after you, since you were involved with Hilda and the sex club."

"I hope not. I'm living a simple lifestyle these days. I'll have another year of intensive therapy with Harry before I recover from my childhood. Good talking to you."

"Sure thing, Phillip. Keep in touch."

❁

SEVENTY-FIVE

It was bright, sunny, and cool the second Saturday in January. A cold front had spread all the way out into the Gulf the day before. Barbara's front beds were a riot of color with flowering kale and pansies.

"I didn't know you were a gardener," Helen commented, as Barbara greeted her at the front door.

"I'm not, I had the nursery come do it. There are things I like that I would never get around to doing, so it's worth the money. I hope ya'll like lunch. I'm not much of a cook, spent all my time in labs and libraries, but it's hard to ruin a pot of veggie soup."

"Super! Just what we need on a winter day," said Clare.

"So what's new?" asked Barbara.

"I have something to share," Trish said as she produced a letter-sized, manila envelope. "I just received this from Phillip Atwater in yesterday's mail. There was a cover letter from him saying he received it just a few days ago. The postmark was Key West."

"Don't keep us in suspense! Who is it from?" asked Helen.

"You'll know. Let me read it to you. There's no heading. "'This is sent to you because I believe you loved Hilda Rasberry and, as such, are a person who deserves an explanation of events that led to her untimely death.

"'I first met Hilda, of all things, while taking out the garbage. We became instant friends, and although I'm shy by nature, she was jolly and made me laugh. She didn't think anything bad about my masculine appearance, because it wasn't long before she was making sexual comments about how she was sexually aroused when around me.

"'That awakened a sexual drive I never knew I was capable of and resulted in our having a flaming affair. I do not consider it lesbian, because I feel like a man in a woman's body. This was after I stopped seeing you. Life was so wonderful. I began to get out more. I volunteered for more garden work.

"'Hilda introduced me to the wider world of plants, as she introduced me to the world of sex in many varieties. She suggested, and I was her slave. We engaged in "special sessions," as she called them, at her sex club where patrons had special requests that required more than one person.

"'I used to do her hair for her, touch up the roots, in her kitchen. It was a fun, close time. At least it was for me. I became her confidant, I thought, especially when she began to ask me to deliver envelopes, which I suspected contained money, to a person on a street corner, at different times.

"'I knew she saw men, but I was fully convinced we were soul mates, and I was Mr. Wonderful to her—until I did a money drop sometime in early July. The turd from New Orleans who took the envelope informed me that Hilda was closing the sex club and getting married. When he said your name, Dr. Phillip Atwater, I really lost it. I slammed that SOB up against the wall, called him a liar and walked off.

"'Doubts came into my mind. Dr. Atwater, you were the therapist I saw for depression for months, and when I thought of you and Hilda—the more I thought about it, the angrier I became. I went from hurt to rage. Of course, I felt compelled to hear it from Hilda herself.

"'All my dreams down the tube. I had been so thrilled with the prospect of living fully as the man I was born to be. I felt strong, and the mirror told me my muscles were impressive. All I needed was the breast reduction surgery.

"'I called Hilda the night she died and said I had some tools to return to her. I had them to use on a Green Garden Gang project. She said she had something to tell me.

"'I entered by the back door. She had given me a key when our relationship became intense, and I leaned the shovel against the wall beside the door. I asked her if it was true that she was marrying another man. She said, "I'm marring a man." I was furious. What was I to her? What about all the pledges of love and trust and being soul mates? What about that? I couldn't believe she was so callous and cold. The bitch had the nerve to look me in the eye and say 'I lied.' I said, 'Are you lying to this man you are marrying?' 'Maybe so,' she said. "I think not, though. What he and I have is definitely different than our relationship."

"'How mean. I felt lower than a snake's belly, and I'm sure it showed. It dawned on me with a clear realization that Hilda liked to see others suffer. She was a bloody sadist. I then realized she was probably lying to you also, Dr. Atwater, and when something better came along, she would do the same thing to you she did to me.

"'I felt cold detachment descend over me, like nothing was real. I flashed back to childhood beatings and the abuse I'd suffered, when the only way to survive was to detach. But, this was different. I was detached, but aware of a rage I'd never experienced before. She said "'You'd better leave now, Tommie Sue," and turned her back on me. "Is that all you have to say?" I screamed." She didn't acknowledge me, just slowly walked toward the doorway to the living room.

"'I grabbed the shovel beside the back door and smashed her head with all my strength. She went down like a sack of potatoes. Clump. When I realized what I had done, my mind began to race. My first thought was fingerprints. I retrieved from the kitchen drawer the latex gloves I used when tinting Hilda's hair and wiped anywhere I thought my prints might have been. If I couldn't have her, no one would. I turned off all the lights and carried Hilda's body out the back and put her on the rear seat of my car. Again, the rage rose in my throat. I went back to the kitchen and selected a large kitchen knife.

There was no one around so I went back, picked up the shovel and put it in the car, locking her back door behind me.

"'What to do? What to do? I once again felt cold and detached, my rage tempered by the shovel blow. As I drove around in circles, I thought, "God, she wasn't very heavy. How could she walk out on me like that? I've got to get rid of her body. Someplace unrelated to me.

"'Then I remembered the keys to the mental health clinic in the glove box, where I had tossed them last spring after finding them in my pocket. No one would connect me to that place. I remembered going inside on a Saturday with some other women on the gang and going upstairs to find a toilet, as there was a line downstairs, and I couldn't wait. I'd seen a large bathtub in that toilet. I decided to dump her there.

"'It was about midnight when I pulled up close to the back entrance to the clinic. The cleaning crew long gone, the only light inside came from dim security lights at each end of the halls. Taking out the keys, I opened the door, disengaged the alarm with its key, and propped the door open with the shovel. Retrieving Hilda's body, I thought how good it was that I worked out with heavy weights every week, even though she surely didn't weigh over 115 pounds. I took the elevator to the second floor and carried her into the toilet, turning on the light inside. For a moment, I felt a little sorry for Hilda when I saw her in the light, and as I laid her in the tub on her back, her hair caught on the faucet. She was a bluish color, and I thought she was dead.

"'Then I remembered I had the knife tucked into the back of my waistband. When I realized again what I had lost, a rage like an erupting volcano overcame me. I burned white-hot as I slashed her throat with all my strength. I was surprised to see blood spurt out. I jumped back, carefully wrapping the knife in paper towels, replacing it in my waistband, I turned off the light, and returned to the back exit.

"'As I started to reset the alarm, I noticed I had used the shovel to prop open the door. What to do with it? The door under the stairs that led to a crawl storage area was convenient. I moved several empty cardboard boxes, opened the door, and stashed the shovel inside, under the steps. Replacing the boxes and resetting the alarm, I left. I saw no cars as I left the parking lot.

"'I wanted you to know, Dr. Atwater, because by the time you read this I'll be in a better place. Thomas Brantley.'"

"Wow!" exhaled Helen.

"I don't believe it!" said Clare.

"I wonder if she's dead?" said Trish. "I'll call Clyde. He can check on deaths in Key West, the postmark on Phillip's package."

Trish set the phone down. "Clyde said it wouldn't take long to check on any suicides or violent deaths in Key West. I gave him this number."

"Well, we had some of it right," said Clare. "Strange as she was, I didn't suspect her of murder."

"I was thinking," said Trish, "if old Judge Neville were here, he would quote William Congreve, saying, 'Hell hath no fury like a woman scorned.' That's for sure here."

The phone rang. It was Clyde.

"What did he say?" asked Clare.

"He said a Tom Brantley was found dead of an apparent overdose of imipramine, a tricyclic antidepressant. Female body with male ID, in an alley behind a local watering hole."

"That's the end of our mystery, or rather tragedy," said Helen.

"One last thing," said Trish. "Helen, do you have the number for Margaret from the Green Garden Gang, who was on the work force with Tommie Sue?"

"Sure, it's in the Garden Club yearbook. But it'll be in the phone book. What's this about?"

"I want to ask her a question."

"Margaret, sorry to bother you. Trish McLeod here. I'm a friend of Helen's, you call her Prissy. She said you had worked with a Tommie Sue Brantley on a garden crew. Do you remember her? Great. Could you say whether she was right- or left-handed. You're sure? Thanks."

Trish put down the phone. "Tommie Sue didn't kill her."

"What?" the other three exclaimed.

"Margaret said they all signed a sheet of paper, a role, to certify that each person had worked on a project. She remembered that Tommie Sue was left-handed, because she signed after her, and there was fumbling as she took the pen. The autopsy report indicated the fatal slash was done by a person who was right-handed."

"Jesus!" said Clare. "We're back to square one."

"Maybe not," said Trish. "Maybe Tommie Sue hit Hilda with the shovel and pushed someone against that wall, but there was another person, the real killer, who committed the actual murder with the slash."

"How long was it," asked Helen, "from the time the fellow from New Orleans told Tommie Sue that Hilda was closing the club and getting married, until the time Hilda was killed?"

"It couldn't have been more than three or four days."

"She said she did it in the letter," said Barbara.

"We don't even know if Tommie Sue actually wrote that letter. We know she had depression in the past. Phillip had treated her with antidepressants, and Hilda's death was a big loss in her life, whether she killed her or was an accessory," said Trish.

"So, another person, the killer, could have written the letter?"

"Why would Tommie Sue write that she did it when she didn't?" said Helen.

"When patients relate traumatic events, there's frequently a mixture of fact and fiction," commented Clare.

"I say Tommie Sue hooked up with this person, and he helped her take Hilda to the clinic. From what she wrote, I believe she hit Hilda with the shovel, but if she was left-handed, she didn't slash her throat."

"What kind of person would slash a dead body?"

"A person who hated women and had fantasies of mutilation, or a person who could tell she wasn't dead and saw a need to finish the job."

"Well, I'm totally confused at this point," said Helen.

"Join the group," said Clare. "All we can do now is to see if Clyde can check if there was any doubt surrounding Tommie Sue's suicide. She must have written the letter to Phillip before taking the pills. She might have written what she did to Phillip to close the door on the affair and protect the killer."

"Why would she do that?"

"I haven't a clue," said Trish. "Maybe a long weekend in Key West would be nice, just Steven and me. My mother has been dying to keep the baby for a few days."

"What would you do there, Trish?"

"I have no idea, sit in the sun, sip mimosas, and listen to whatever I hear. I think Steven will go for it. He needs a break, and the sailing and fishing are good."

"Do you think Tommie Sue was in Key West all these months?" said Helen.

"It sure looks that way. Remember, she probably looked very much like a man, especially if she had the breast surgery," said Barbara.

"That surgery isn't complicated, and if she had it shortly after Hilda's death, she would have been able to work. She probably paid cash for the surgery, in a month or so, when she'd saved enough money," said Clare.

"And," said Helen, "there are quite a few elderly rich people who would be glad to pay cash for the services of a good physical therapist."

"She was taking testosterone, so someone had to write a prescription," said Trish.

"Not necessarily," said Clare. "You can buy most anything off the internet these days. The ID on her body was male, so it must not have taken much to get that. Why not any drug she wanted?"

Helen interjected, "Do we think she was a druggie, too?"

"Somehow, I don't think so, maybe some alcohol and anti-depressants. Of course, they don't mix either. She certainly was unhappy and depressed, and testosterone can affect the mind also, depending on how much she took, and if we add in anabolic steroids, another possibility, that would explain short-temper, anger, and rage outbreaks for sure."

"Are you going to tell Steven why you want a little trip to Key West?" asked Barbara.

"Maybe later," said Trish.

SEVENTY-SIX

It was still high season when Trish made the reservations for a guest house in Old Town.

"For a while I was afraid we weren't going to get anything; everyone and his cat must want Key West this winter. It certainly has changed since I was a child."

"Probably all the cruise ship crowd," said Steven. "That's part of it, but Old Town still has some charm."

"Now if we have some steady, good sailing weather for three days, I'll be a happy man."

"Oh, Steven, you're a happy man anyway."

"Thanks and we can just hole up in our bedroom if it rains."

"We'll see," said Trish, smiling.

"Ready for a walk?"

"Sure thing," said Trish. "Let's even do the tourist thing and ride the Conch Train."

The next evening, after a morning sail, a post-lunch nap, and browsing a few boutiques, dinner at Pepe's was the end of a lovely day.

"What are you doing tomorrow?" asked Trish.

"I've called my old fishing buddy, John, and so we'll be heading out early. You won't be too lonely, will you?"

"Me? You're kidding. I'll browse more shops. Maybe look for some needlework. I'll keep myself entertained...do some sleuthing. I have a nice thick paperback. How about supper at the place? The kitchen looks well stocked. Do you need the car?"

"No, John will pick me up, so it's all yours. Please be careful."

"Not to worry, Steven. Maybe we'll just cook what you catch."

"Better not count on that."

Trish decided to stop by the library and read the brief newspaper account of Tommie Sue's death.

Not much here, she said to herself, but she/he did live in Old Town. I'll just jot down the address.

Later Trish entered a small shop a block from the address.

"May I help you?" The clerk, a stout, middle-aged woman with dark Mediterranean looks, stepped from behind a curtain of beads. She was dressed in a colorful, big shirt and gauzy pants that accented her bulk. She jingled as she moved from long earrings and assorted bracelets.

"Just browsing, thanks," said Trish. "Nice shop. Are you the owner?"

"Yes, I am."

"Oh, how's business this year?"

"Not bad, could be better. You like?" She gestured to a half sheet seascape watercolor.

"That is nice," Trish said. "You live around here?"

"Sure do. Have my place right in back of the shop."

"This a pretty quiet area?"

"Generally. We have a little trouble every now and then, but it's a low crime area."

"That was too bad about the suicide of Tom or Tommie Sue Brantley. The paper said it happened just down the street from here."

"I never would have dreamed he was a she. In fact, he bought a watercolor from me for his place. In my view he was a sad, angry fellow, not much for words. We have a fair number of gay couples that live and winter here, but they're mostly regular folk. Not cross-dressers like he was."

"Did he live alone?"

"Far as I know, he did. I only sold him the painting and

saw him on the street a couple of times. Said hello. That's about it. Did you know him or anything?"

"No, the name came up in conversation back home. He lived on the Gulf Coast before moving down here. He had seen a friend of mine for depression."

"He just commented that he needed some pictures on the walls in his place. He sure never looked happy when I saw him on the street, and that was only maybe two or three times. I have a high school girl help out on Saturdays and some days after school. Otherwise, I'm pretty much here during shop hours. It's sad. You never know the troubles people have and they go and kill themselves like that."

"Would you happen to know who the landlord is for that address?"

"No, but the people are friendly here. You could just knock and ask."

"Thanks, I will."

Trish decided to talk to a realtor on the phone rather than door knocking. Back at the guest house, after twenty minutes' chat with a lady realtor who wanted to sell her a condo, she finally asked about rental in Old Town and was informed that Jack Wray was the man to talk to about properties in Old Town.

Talk about luck. Jack's agency managed several properties in the area. When asked about the address for Tommie Sue, he said they handled it, but it was just a week ago that it was leased to a nice couple from Detroit, for three months.

"Oh," said Trish. "Did you know Tommie Sue Brantley?"

"You mean Tom Brantley?"

"Yes," replied Trish. "He was an acquaintance on the coast where he lived prior to here. We were saddened to hear of his death."

Liar, liar, said Trish's inner voice.

"I can't say much, except the rent was always paid in cash. The reason I remember is it's a little unusual around here. Most write a check."

"Did you happen to know what kind of work he did?"

"I think some sort of physical therapy or massage, I'm not sure."

"Well, thanks. By the way, did ya'll clean out the place after he died? Were there any relatives?"

"No relatives we knew about. After the police took a look and said they found several medicine bottles, we had our regular maintenance people clean it up. It wasn't bad, anyway. Hardly anything in there except a few clothes and toiletries—shaver, Old Spice aftershave. No books, a few TV dinners in the freezer compartment. I told the maintenance guy to take it. We usually let them have anything left behind when renters leave."

"Did you ever see anyone else around?"

"Come to think of it, there was one gentleman, a little older than he was. Very spiffy, expensive casual clothes, like Italian. I saw him several times over the months Tom lived there. A couple of times when they were leaving, I thought they were going out to dinner. The thought crossed my mind that they were a gay couple. The older fellow acted protective."

"Do you have any idea of his name?"

"No, but he drove a silver Rolls, and that's a very expensive car. Don't see many of those around Key West."

"I wouldn't think you'd see many of those around anywhere."

"I agree."

Back at the guesthouse, Trish took a bubble bath while she contemplated her visit to inquire about Tommie Sue's last place to hang her hat.

Damn! What a setback.

"Trish, can I come in?"

"I think I can allow that. After all, it's over a year we've been together. I hate to see a man suffer from an overdistended bladder."

"Sometimes you're too scientific, Trish," said Steven, as he relieved himself in the toilet.

"My, what a big pee, Steven," teased Trish.

"The amount or the instrument? I can be scientific, too. Take it any way you want."

Finished, Steven leaned over to kiss Trish and as he did, she put her arms around his neck and pulled him into the tub, laughing. Laughing, too, Steven said, "This may be the way it is in the movies, but I prefer a nice bed."

"Me, too," agreed Trish.

Dinner at Pepe's was much later than they planned. Over dinner, Steven asked Trish about her day of sleuthing.

"Another dead end, but she/he did have a male friend who drove a silver Rolls. Maybe, back home, my trusty cop, Clyde, can get the names of any registered in the Key West area, and we'll know if one was Ramirez."

Suddenly, Trish paused and exclaimed, "Oh, my God!"

"What's the matter," asked Steven, alarmed.

"I forgot my birth control pills. I haven't had one in three days."

"Oh, ho, ho," said Steven. "Maybe you won't be going back to the medical center after all. Would you mind?"

"Of course not."

"We'll see. Let's enjoy the rest of our stay, anyway. "You're on, Big Boy," Trish grinned.

"I better find a copy of Kama Sutra with you talking like that," retorted Steven.

❀

SEVENTY-SEVEN

"Good trip, Dr. Trish?" Clyde's now familiar voice came over the phone.

"Great, Clyde. Say, can you trace a certain type of car for me in Florida?"

"Sure, what's up?"

Trish related visiting Tommie Sue's last address and the conversation with the manager. "Since that's not a common car, I thought we might find the name of any owners in, say, the Keys, specifically Key West."

"You're at home these days?"

"Yes."

"I'll call you if I find anything."

Next, Trish quickly called Barbara at school.

"It was pretty pitiful where Tommie Sue lived. Not a classy joint by any means."

"Any leads?"

"Only that she/he had a male friend who drove a very expensive car like the one Steven and I saw John Ramirez get into."

"So, maybe the police need to talk to him."

"They probably wouldn't, unless we have some additional information. They wrote his/her death off as a suicide, remember? Barb, how well do you know McInnis, the coroner?"

"He comes to grand rounds every now and then, especially if it has forensic implications."

"I knew him slightly when I was a resident. He was just

finishing his pathology residency. Do you think he would listen to what we four gals have been discussing or tell me any details of the autopsy?"

"I think he might, Trish. He's a bit of a grouch publicly, but, hell, they hardly give him any money to do the job. It's a miracle he accomplishes as much as he does. Want his home number?"

"Sure. I'll call him tonight and get back with you. We might need to have another gal group meeting."

SEVENTY-EIGHT

That afternoon, while the baby was asleep, Trish grabbed her pocket phone book on an impulse and called Phillip Atwater.

"How's it going, Phil?"

"Good to hear your voice, Trish. It's a good thing you called now. I've joined the Episcopal Church and have applied for admission to a religious community, so I probably wouldn't be able to talk to you for a while."

"Well, that's a shock. A religious community like a monastery? Are you sure?"

"This is the happiest I've ever been in my life. I think I've found my true calling."

"I'm happy for you. Listen, Phil, Tommie Sue couldn't have killed Hilda. Yep, I'm sure. I'll talk to McInnis, the coroner, tonight and see if I can get any further details. You saw her for about six to seven months, right?"

It was thirty minutes later when Trish replaced the receiver, saying under her breath, "Well, Smoke, that explains a lot."

Smoke blinked his blue eyes and replied with a meow.

SEVENTY-NINE

"This is Trish McLeod. I was an acquaintance of Dr. McInnis back when we were in residency. Is he available for a quick professional question or two?"

"Hi, Trish," boomed Bert McInnis. "Sure, I remember you. What's up?"

Trish quickly shared her thoughts and the letter Phillip Atwater had received.

"You're correct, Trish. The slash to the throat, 100% sure, came from a right-handed person."

"I saw the body in the tub. Ghastly, but I didn't notice a lot of blood outside the tub. Oh, a little blood outside the tub? Anything unusual? Ever see that before? Did you keep samples? Sorry I asked. I know better than that.

"Thanks a bunch. I'm sure the police will let you know if you need to run DNA on the specimen. I realize it's strange for a shrink like me to get involved in a case like this, but seeing her body was a major trauma for me, and I've developed an insatiable curiosity about her death."

It was a few days later when Clyde called to report only one car of that color and make was registered in Key West. "You're lucky it was such an expensive car."

"You're sure of the name?"

"Yep, Dr. John Ramirez."

"Time for me to make an appointment with the detective on Hilda's case, Bill Swanson."

"Say, Dr. Trish, don't let him know how much I've helped. I mean, don't mention my name."

EIGHTY

It was midsummer and afternoon heat simmered on the distant gray Gulf. Behind the wall of sliding glass doors, a festive baby shower was in progress.

"You two may have had a late start, but you're making up for lost time," said Helen.

Trish laughed, "I think we'll stop now. This one's a girl."

"So, they're bringing John Ramirez to trial?" asked Clare.

"It's so exciting that we were a part of solving the crime. I just hate that this excitement is associated with such a terrible murder," drawled Helen.

"What nailed it down, Trish?" said Barbara.

"It was several things. When I shared the letter from Tommie Sue with the coroner and told him John Ramirez had been seen in the company of Tommie Sue in Key West, that was enough for him to remind the police of his unusual finding on the body, a glob of mucous, as if the killer cleared his throat and spat on her. So, they ran the DNA and sure enough, it was matched to Ramirez.

"It's amazing to me how a fellow as intelligent as he is in some ways, is so dumb in others. The police found the knife in his kitchen in Key West. It had been cleaned, but not in a dishwasher, so there was enough material to run DNA on it. Even after such a long time, it matched Hilda's."

"But what about the letter from Tommie Sue?" Helen asked.

"Ramirez was Hilda's special client and had been for several years. He was at Hilda's when she told Tommie Sue and him that she was out of the sex business and making a new life with Phillip. Tommie Sue bashed Hilda with the shovel, and Ramirez helped take the body to the clinic. Tommie Sue probably didn't know Hilda was still alive or that Ramirez was going to kill her, but she saw it."

"So, how come she wrote the letter saying she did it?" said Clare.

"Phillip Atwater told me Tommie Sue had severe childhood psychic trauma, that she had episodes where she dissociated under stress. Ramirez convinced her she had committed the crime. He filled her with details until she believed everything she wrote Phillip in that letter. Ramirez was in a rage that Hilda was cutting him off from whatever special jollies she provided. Police are re-investigating the case of the post doc fellow from his department who was stabbed to death at the medical school."

"Poor Tommie Sue was just a pawn," said Helen, as a crack of lightning and a loud boom of thunder rattled the glass doors.

A storm swept in from the Gulf, drenching the wide deck and washing it clean of scattered debris. In one corner, a crumbled business card rode a stream of water. It read, "Notti's, Where More Is Not Enough."

❁

ABOUT THE AUTHOR

Fran Hagaman is a retired professor of clinical psychiatry, LSU Medical School, Shreveport, and a distinguished fellow of the American Psychiatric Association. She also served as Medical Director of Region 7 Louisiana Mental Health. She is a longtime associate member of the SW Chapter of Mystery Writers of America. Fran lives in Shreveport, Lousiana.

Also Available:

Ding Dong Bell - Death in a Stairwell

A Medical Mystery

Trish McLeod mysteries can be ordered
from fine bookstores everywhere.

❃

To contact the author email:
Fran@Hagaman.com